D0070419

GREEN FIRE

•

Victoria Sheringham

AVALON BOOKS
NEW YORK

PRINTED IN THE UNITED STATES OF AMERICA
ON ACID-FREE PAPER
BY HADDON CRAFTSMEN, BLOOMSBURG,
PENNSYLVANIA

For my grandmother, Rose Evelyn Kennedy

"The man in the wilderness asked me
How many strawberries grew in the sea?
I answered him as I thought good,
As many as red herrings grew in the wood."

Chapter One

Caitlin stared in stunned silence at the wrought iron gates blocking the driveway. In all the summers she had spent visiting her great-aunt and uncle, the gates had never been closed.

Always propped open in welcome, the tall stone posts and black metal gates were the family joke, a grand entrance to the Hughes estate—which consisted only of a small log cabin. Now, after the fire, they were all that was left of the family homestead.

Slowing her car, Caitlin pulled over to the

side of the road, a cloud of dust engulfing the small trailer she towed. The quiet slam of the car door echoed in the stillness as she approached the gate, hoping it wasn't locked. The cold metal swung easily on its hinges. Caitlin pushed the doors wide and secured them in their usual place.

The familiar view down the driveway cheered Caitlin immediately. The peaks of the dark and distant Olympic mountains were still dusted with snow. The gray water of the Strait of Juan de Fuca was frosted with white caps, and a strong sea breeze welcomed Caitlin back to the island.

The last time she had visited had been such a blur of emotions and duties, Caitlin could hardly believe it was only two months ago. It had been easier then, surrounded by her parents and her three cousins. They had all clustered together and comforted each other in their grief.

Somehow Caitlin still expected Aunt Elizabeth would be here to greet her, just as she had on every other visit.

Inching her car down the narrow drive, burdened with the trailer and all her belongings, Caitlin carefully avoided looking at the blackened ruins lying just out of sight. She came to a halt as far from the remains of the old cabin as she could and backed the trailer onto a level, sunny spot.

Once out of the car, Caitlin knew she couldn't ignore the charred remains of the cabin. Even the air held the faint smell of smoke, ominous after so many months. Taking a deep breath to steady her emotions, Caitlin moved back toward the old Hughes homestead.

Staring at the burnt timbers and the crumbling foundation, Caitlin felt the tears roll down her cheeks. Never in all her dreams had she expected Aunt Elizabeth and Uncle Emmet would bequeath her the family home, and the ten-acre parcel of waterfront property.

The family had known Aunt Elizabeth and Uncle Emmet had done well in selling off their waterfront land over the years, but the size of the estate had been overwhelming. Caitlin was still dazed by the will. Her cousins had received enough money to make their lives very secure, but Caitlin had received the most precious gift of all: the remaining land where her ancestors had settled.

Looking past the devastation of the cabin, Caitlin's gaze fell on the flowerbeds. Crushed by the Otter Creek Volunteer Fire Department's trucks, only an ancient peony remained. Bending to inhale the fragrant white bloom, Caitlin let warm memories of happy childhood summers wash away her grief. Holidays on Vancouver Island had always been magical.

"Don't worry, Uncle Emmet. I will restore your gardens as soon as I can." It was only whispered to the peony but Caitlin looked around to make sure she was alone. It had seemed normal talking to herself on the long drive out, but now she was home.

The word, *home*, startled Caitlin. Aunt Elizabeth had always encouraged her to pursue her dream of becoming an architect. Now Caitlin had a chance to fulfill her second dream, building a home of her own.

A wave of doubt washed over her as she looked at her little green car—now gray with dust from her journey—and the small trailer that would be home while she built. Maybe she was a fool to abandon everyone and everything to attempt something completely new on her own.

It was one thing to be able to design on paper. It was a completely different process to actually try and build one of her own designs herself.

Caitlin shrugged off her fears. She was tired of waiting for some Prince Charming to come and sweep her off her feet. She had been waiting, however unconsciously, for too long. Now, at twenty-five, it was time to take her fate into her own hands. Caitlin's only regret was that it had taken Aunt Elizabeth's death to jolt her into living.

She shivered despite the warm June day

as a cloud drifted in front of the sun. A sudden sound startled Caitlin from her reveries. She was surprised to find a tall, fair-haired man watching her.

Her pulse still pounding from the unexpected visitor, she stammered, "I didn't hear a car . . ." She paused to collect herself. "Sorry, I meant to say hello."

The man smiled, and Caitlin found herself mirroring his grin.

"Hello. You must be Elizabeth's niece." He extended his hand. "I'm Kyle Dermott. I'm your tenant."

"Tenant?" Caitlin's voice trailed off in confusion. The cabin was burnt beyond habitation, her trailer was only eleven-feet long, and the rest of the property was woodland and lawn. *Where could Kyle Dermott possibly live?* His grin told her he understood her dilemma.

He pointed out to the waters of the Strait of Juan de Fuca. "Your aunt let me moor in the cove. I have the *Sea Unicorn* tied up below the cliff. I'm so sorry about Elizabeth's death, she was a very special and independent lady."

Caitlin had to laugh at the understatement. She appreciated his sympathy and his understanding of Aunt Elizabeth. Her stubbornness and independence had worried her family, but they had allowed her to stay on in the cabin after Uncle Emmet's death ten years ago.

Caitlin found herself liking Kyle Dermott. There was something warm and comforting in his handshake, and his smile was open and honest. She would have guessed he was the outdoor type just from his tanned complexion and the rugged air about him.

"I hope we can come to terms so I can continue to use the dock. There are very few deep water coves in this area. And don't worry, it's not permanent, I head south to Mexico every winter."

Caitlin nodded, suddenly growing shy as she realized she was still shaking his hand. Even worse, she had not made a proper introduction. She hadn't said anything except an awkward hello. Releasing his hand, she said, "I'm Caitlin Hughes. Whatever arrangement you had with Aunt Elizabeth is fine with me."

"You'd like me to continue to do your grocery shopping and laundry?" Kyle raised one eyebrow over twinkling dark eyes.

"Oh, no." Caitlin grew flustered. "I can do that myself! But thank you for looking out for Aunt Elizabeth's needs. Are you a fisherman?"

Kyle laughed. "I don't fish regularly, although I can't resist trying my luck when the salmon are in season. I am a photographer. With so much natural beauty here, there's no shortage of subject matter."

His dark eyes seemed to focus completely on Caitlin and she told herself not to be silly as her heart fluttered slightly. He was obviously referring to the mountains and trees and wildlife, not to her.

Caitlin knew she hardly qualified as a natural beauty with her dark hair cut short and practical, and the odd hazel eyes that changed color depending on her mood. She had been called cute, perky, and even feisty when she demanded her own way on a job site, but never beautiful.

"I see you have a trailer. Are you going to live in it permanently or rebuild?" Kyle's question stirred Caitlin and she was touched by his interest.

"I'm going to build. I have designed the house myself, and I know exactly where I want it." Caitlin pointed to a clearing midway between the cliff and the edge of the trees.

"Every summer, my Uncle Emmet would pitch a tent for me right there. I always said they should have built the cabin there." Caitlin smiled. "But I was so young then, I never really considered how difficult it would have been to just clear the land, or build the cabin."

"And now you can have your chance to rebuild." Kyle's encouragement made Caitlin blush.

She nodded and confessed. "I can build

here now, after spending years learning how to design something for a rocky site." They laughed together at her admission, a sound that seemed to echo across the strait to the distant mountains of the Olympic Peninsula.

The crunch of tires on gravel attracted their attention. A shiny new pickup truck pulled beside Caitlin's little Honda. The truck door slammed as a middle-aged man got out. He pulled his faded baseball cap down over his forehead, and hoisted his jeans up over his thick waist. Raising one hand in greeting, he came toward them.

The man nodded and put out his hand to Kyle. "Simon Duff Contracting. You must be the architect that Hughes girl hired. It won't be easy on this site. Lots of rock, and blasting will be really expensive. No place for the septic field for any house bigger than the cabin that was here. And you sure can't build on that spot, the foundation's too badly burned."

The man's rush of words prevented Kyle from speaking, although he managed to disentangle his hand from the contractor's. The pause was long enough for Caitlin to interrupt.

"We spoke on the phone, Mr. Duff."

He turned to her as if seeing her for the first time. "You must be the secretary I spoke to."

"I am the architect." The coolness of Caitlin's tone did not seem to register with the man.

"Miss Hughes must be a feminist or something to hire a female architect."

Caitlin kept her anger in check, realizing it would do no good to argue with this man's mentality. She chose her words carefully.

"Ms. Hughes believes in the equality of the sexes. A female architect is no different from a male architect. In fact, I do believe Ms. Hughes intends to do the general contracting of this project herself."

Caitlin gave Duff her sweetest smile. "I

am so sorry to have brought you all the way out here, but I don't think I'll need your services after all."

The man stood staring at Caitlin, not believing what he heard. He began to shake his head, angry at her dismissal. "You'll be sorry," he began to mutter. "This site is nothing but trouble."

Caitlin waved cheerily as the man stormed off.

"I'm impressed." Kyle saluted her. "I didn't know male chauvinists like that were still around. You handled him very well."

"Thanks. I'm just glad I didn't hire him. With that kind of attitude, he never would have listened to a woman—architect or not."

Caitlin let her anger drain away, knowing it was useless. She'd learned the hard way that some of the men in the construction trade resented a woman telling them what to do.

"Can you do it?"

"Do what?" Caitlin asked.

"Build the house yourself. I would hate to think he forced you into this situation."

Caitlin ignored the flicker of self-doubt and took a deep breath to steady herself. "Yes. At least I'll give it a try. Now all I really need is someone to help with the general labor."

Kyle grew thoughtful. "Well, I don't know . . . I guess I could follow orders from a woman. Where should I send my résumé?" He paused and added. "Ms. Hughes."

Caitlin had the sense to realize he was teasing and she laughed. "Are you serious?" Caitlin found her heart pounding with excitement. She held her breath as he answered.

"Very serious. Nature photography is a wonderful job but the income isn't very steady. I'm happy to work hard, if you don't mind having to teach me what to do." His grin caused them both to laugh. "Besides, you won't let me shop or do the laundry, but I bet you'll let me dig ditches and pound nails."

"You're right! You're hired." Caitlin shook his hand in agreement. "But you have to let me pay you a fair wage since I intend to work you very hard."

"Done. When do we start?"

"Tomorrow morning, I guess. No sense delaying."

Kyle gave her hand a shake to seal the agreement. "See you in the morning, boss." He gave a brief wave as he disappeared down the steep trail to the dock.

In the growing dark, Caitlin could just see the tops of the *Sea Unicorn's* masts as she returned to the car. The warmth of Kyle's handshake, however businesslike, still filled Caitlin with a faint glow, and a clear image of Kyle's guileless smile flashed in her memory.

The chill in the air sent a shiver down Caitlin's back. The darkening shadows reminded her of the blackened ruins lying just behind her. Simon Duff's muttered threats suddenly seemed loud and menacing in the twilight.

Anxious to prepare her trailer for the night, Caitlin glanced up at the night sky. The twinkle of the first evening star shone like a gem in the heavens. Closing her eyes, she silently wished for a happier ending to her story.

The beauty of the view overwhelmed Caitlin's fears. She let the excitement she first felt about deciding to move bubble through her.

The sense of sadness that had gripped her since she first arrived faded as Caitlin realized Aunt Elizabeth and Uncle Emmet had left her the land for a reason. She made a silent vow in their memory. *A Hughes will live on this land for a long time to come.*

Chapter Two

"Yes, of course I'm going to build. Who told you differently?" Caitlin wanted to smash the receiver down in frustration. "I have no intention of cancelling my order, so please deliver the supplies as I requested."

Caitlin knew she was conspicuous, standing in the lobby of the Cove Resort, shouting into a pay phone at the crack of dawn. Her brand-new work clothes and spotless boots labeled her a novice builder. Thankfully the clerk at the building supply store couldn't see how insecure Caitlin felt.

17

"Are you all right, dear?"

Caitlin gave a little start but was relieved to see a familiar face. "Mrs. Wells. It's good to see you again. I was just getting a few things straightened out before heading back to the lot."

Flo Wells took off her reading glasses. "Ed tells me you're staying in a trailer. You know you're welcome here—not that we've got a cabin to spare. Business is booming."

Caitlin's anger faded with Flo's cheery talk. It probably was simply a mixup at the office. "I noticed you've built more cabins over the past few years. Everything looks great."

Flo nodded happily. "We've discovered the secret—hot tubs! Even a shack will rent if there's a hot tub."

Caitlin laughed. "And I suppose your success has nothing to do with the beautiful view of the beach, or your management."

Mrs. Wells preened at the compliment. "Thank you, dear. It's been a lot of years getting the place up and running. We began our expansion when your aunt sold us the beach acreage. Now it seems to practically run itself. The kids are always after me to retire."

"I'll believe that when I see it." Caitlin had known the Wellses all her life, and she doubted either Flo or Ed could sit idly.

"No, I suppose you're right. I do like to keep busy. And Ed fills his days with so many committees and meetings, they'd never let him retire. The Chamber of Commerce is always signing him up for some project or another. At least it keeps him out of trouble." Flo grew concerned. "I do think you should consider parking your trailer down here. There's electricity and showers, and it would be safer."

"Not to worry, Mrs. Wells. It's safer if I stay on the site. That way no one can steal my wood or supplies." Caitlin held up her hand. "Not that I think anyone would, but building sites are easy targets when no one is there."

"Oh, I never thought of that. Well, you

know best, dear. And you know you're always welcome here. That is the one thing about running a resort—someone is always on duty."

"Thanks, Mrs. Wells. I'll sleep better knowing I have neighbors nearby."

"You've met our Mr. Dermott have you? Handsome devil isn't he?" Flo gave Caitlin a wink that left her laughing.

"I have met him. He's going to help me build the house."

"Now there's a sight I'd like to see, Kyle swinging a hammer. Lucky you. Just make sure you're finished by fall. Once the rains start, he'll be gone to Mexico. Follows the gray whales each winter. Comes back every spring like the robins, all tanned and relaxed."

Caitlin pictured Kyle returning, like a breath of fresh spring air, and her dreamy smile was mirrored by Flo's. Both women laughed and Caitlin shook her head to clear it.

"Then I better get started if Kyle has a

deadline. I'll see you next time I need to use your phone."

"Anytime, dear. I miss Elizabeth's visits every morning. After she walked the beach, she would join me for a cup of coffee. Can I tempt you with one today?"

"Your donuts are even more tempting, but I'll save them both for another day."

"I wish I had your will power. I've been baking and eating them for years. A good thing I am naturally skinny or I'd never fit behind this counter." Mrs. Wells went back to her reading as Caitlin headed for the beach trail.

The steep climb back to the lot left Caitlin winded, and she marveled at Aunt Elizabeth's stamina. Her daily walks were legendary in the family. City life had left Caitlin soft, but building would whip her into shape in no time.

Avoiding the sight of the blackened ruins, Caitlin hurried to her trailer. She found her new shovel beneath a pile of assorted tools.

Grabbing a tape measure, she went over to the area she'd marked out for her house. She smiled at the thought. *Her house*, what lovely words.

She lifted her boot and broke the ground with a firm shove. As she flung the dirt away, she noticed a similar pile of rubble nearby. Dropping the shovel, Caitlin walked over to the dirt and stared into a freshly dug hole.

Confused, she looked around and was astounded to see similar holes all around her. They must have been dug over a long period of time. Most holes were bone dry but many were still damp. Caitlin stared at the ruined lawn. She had intended to seed the area with wildflowers eventually, but the holes lay like ugly sores amongst the green grass.

The frightening part was, someone had been very deliberately digging on her land. A sudden rustle of the underbrush caused Caitlin's heart to beat rapidly. She whirled around to stare into the woods behind her. Had someone been watching her?

She glanced to the cliff edge, hoping to see Kyle arriving for work. The sound of movement made Caitlin turn back to the brush as something crashed nearby.

"Come out right now, or I'll charge you with trespassing." Caitlin's voice echoed across the empty site. It sounded much braver than she felt. She considered it might only be a deer, but she held her breath as she heard more rustling.

She stifled a scream as something bounded out of the trees. It stood wagging its tail, its long pink tongue hanging out eagerly, brown eyes fixed on Caitlin, waiting for her next command.

Her heart pounding, Caitlin put her hand out for the dog to sniff. Golden brown and white, it looked like some kind of spaniel. Its stump of a tail wagged ridiculously, sending the long white curls on the end waving in the wind.

"Are you a nice dog, or did you dig all these holes in my lawn?" The dog pressed its nose into her palm and danced away, happily running in circles.

"Taffy!" A small voice called from the woods. "Here girl! Taffy!" The dog stopped its leaping and ran toward the little girl in the trees.

Caitlin turned with a wave. "Hello. Are you my neighbor?"

The girl stepped forward and nodded. Dressed in denim overalls and a red top, Caitlin guessed she was about five or six. Her light brown hair was tied back in a neat braid.

"What's your name?"

"Pippa. What's yours?"

"Caitlin. I am going to be build a house here . . . did you know my Aunt Elizabeth?"

The little girl nodded. "Yes, my Mom and I went shopping lots for her. Were you very sad about the fire?" Caitlin nodded. "Me too. Now that you live here can I come visit you?"

Caitlin laughed at Pippa's directness. "Of course, but you must only come to visit me in the trailer and not go near the new house until it's finished. While I'm building, you have to promise not to play near it. There are too many things that could cause an accident if we're not careful."

Pippa stood watching Caitlin with big blue eyes. Slowly she nodded as if she had considered each of Caitlin's words and weighed them carefully. "I won't go near your new house 'til you say so, just like I don't go near the old house."

Caitlin smiled at the girl. "Your mom must be very proud of you."

"I am."

Caitlin looked up. Just as a woman emerged from the woods, Pippa rushed over to grab the woman's hand, dragging her toward Caitlin.

"This is Caitlin. She's building a house."

"Hi. I'm Sara Fraser. It's nice to meet you finally. Elizabeth spoke of you and your cousins often." She shook Caitlin's hand.

Standing side by side, there was no mistaking Sara and Pippa as anything but mother and daughter, with their matching blue eyes and brown hair. Caitlin was delighted at the thought of having such friendly neighbors.

"Pippa tells me you helped my aunt with her shopping. That was very kind of you. It was hard on my family to be so far away, worrying about her health after my uncle's death." Caitlin paused as her grief surfaced.

Sara touched her arm. "Elizabeth was very happy. Her only worry was that she would have to leave her home as she grew older. She was very active right 'til the end. We were on the way to our quilting meeting when her chest pains first began so we rushed to the hospital."

Caitlin wiped her cheeks and nodded. "The doctor said she died in her sleep during the night . . . I don't suppose our living closer would have changed her death. We were very grateful for your kindness to her."

"I was sorry to miss the funeral and the chance to meet your family. I had to take Pippa to see her grandparents in England."

Caitlin shook her head. "No need to apologize. You were there when Elizabeth needed you most. I just don't understand the fire . . . how did the cabin burn down if my aunt was in the hospital?"

Sara's blue eyes grew dark with sorrow. "It was such a shock. I'm glad Elizabeth was spared having to deal with it. Does that sound callous?"

"No. In a way it's a small gift that she died before learning everything was lost. I shouldn't say everything is gone—she has given me a great gift." She turned to watch Pippa and Taffy wrestle in the grass. "It's a nice feeling to be on land that's been in my family for so long. Despite earlier generations being gone, I still feel connected to my past." Caitlin grew embarrassed. "Sorry to grow so maudlin on you."

Sara held up her hand. "Never apologize about the past. I work at the museum in town. I spend whole days digging through the days gone by, wondering what it was like. Anything you need to know about Otter Creek's history, give me a call. Your aunt told you about the letters she donated, didn't she?"

Caitlin shook her head but felt a surge of excitement. "Letters? About the Hughes family?"

Catching her enthusiasm, Sara nodded. "Just before the fire, she gave me a bundle of old letters from Emmet's grandfather," Sara paused to calculate, "your great-great-grandfather?"

Too excited to speak, Caitlin nodded.

Sara continued. "They were letters she found buried under some floorboards in the cabin. She thought the museum would like them."

"Have you read them?"

"Not yet. When I last saw them, they were still sitting in "Acquisitions," which is what

Violet Gibbons, the museum director, insists on calling the shelf in our tiny office for newly acquired artifacts."

Caitlin could tell from Sara's tone that Violet Gibbons liked giving fancy titles to minor things. "You must enjoy working there."

"Oh, I love the museum but I could do without Violet."

Pippa called their attention to Kyle, who was coming up the cliff path.

Ready to work, he was dressed in faded denim—but Caitlin laughed when she saw his work boots were as new as her own.

"Morning, Sara. Have you come to give a glowing recommendation to my new employer?"

Sara gave a gentle laugh and inclined her head to Caitlin. "You'll be in safe hands with Kyle. Unless whales or eagles go by—then he is likely to drop his tools and grab his camera." Both women laughed as Kyle smiled.

Sara called Pippa over. "We have to get to work ourselves. The garden is exploding

with weeds. Wait 'til the end of summer—
I'll have more zucchini than I can give away.
It comes with a ten-page recipe booklet,
'10,000 ways to Stuff, Bake, Freeze, and Dis-
guise an Abundance of Zucchini.' I wrote it
myself to try and bribe people to take some
of my surplus."

"I'll consider that a warning. If the house
is done, I'll have room for a few."

"It's a deal. Come along, Pippa. We have
to plant more zucchinis since Caitlin says
she'll take some. And let's make sure Taffy
follows us home—I don't think Caitlin
needs *her* help today."

Waving good-bye, Caitlin gathered her
shovel.

"Have you already started digging?" Kyle
pointed to all the scattered piles of dirt.

Caitlin shook her head. "It wasn't me. I
think Taffy has been digging for bones. But
now that I'm on the site, I can chase her
away. Besides there will be plenty of dirt to
fill in all the holes once we start excavating.
This morning, I just want to lay out rough

foundation lines. With any luck, my wood order will be here by this afternoon."

Kyle must have sensed her mood. "Was there trouble?"

Caitlin shrugged away her worry. "Someone cancelled my order this morning but I straightened it out. I'm not giving up hope yet."

"Good. Where do we start?" Kyle looked around the site then held up his hand. "Listen."

Caitlin didn't hear anything unusual at first. But suddenly a distinct blowing sound carried across the water. She turned to Kyle with a knowing laugh.

"Whales! Now that's the best sign we could ask for on the first day of a new project. Do you want to get your camera?"

Kyle shook his head but Caitlin had already moved toward the cliff. "I used to spend whole summers watching for the Orcas. My Uncle Emmet always said they bring good luck."

She watched in delight as first one, then

two tall black dorsal fins rose out of the waves. The Strait was dotted with the black and white of their cresting heads and fins as the pod spread out chasing the salmon.

Imagining her house complete, with a huge bay window facing the water, she motioned to the grass around her. With a laugh, Caitlin turned to Kyle. "Would you like to join me in my living room?"

Chapter Three

Exhausted after two full days of work, Caitlin flopped back on the narrow bench in her kitchen. It was almost dark but she was too tired to even think about cooking dinner. She decided to heat up some soup later, if she grew hungry. For now, she just wanted to close her eyes and rest.

Caitlin had known building was going to be hard work, but every bone in her body was protesting. Yet the effort involved was worth it—she finally felt like things were underway.

33

Working with Kyle was a dream. He followed her instructions without question. When they came to something she didn't know, they figured out the answer together. There were plenty of challenges ahead but Kyle's good-natured help would make it easier.

Caitlin was thrilled at their progress. They had finished laying out the foundation and were now ready to dig. The excavator was parked in the middle of the building site for an early start in the morning.

All of the lumber had arrived and was neatly stacked to the side of the driveway. Caitlin's aching muscles reminded her of moving every board.

She forced herself to sit up, and groaned as she tugged off her filthy work boots. She no longer looked or felt like a novice builder. Hoping the rest of her wasn't as dirty as her boots, she decided on a shower before eating.

The main reason she had bought this particular trailer, despite its small size, was the shower stall. The bathroom itself was tiny, with one blindingly bright lightbulb, but the hot-water tank was large enough for a decent shower.

Caitlin opened the small frosted window to prevent the room from becoming fogged. Outside the darkness almost hummed with quiet. It felt strange to be so far from the constant city noises she was used to hearing.

After carefully folding up her work clothes, Caitlin stepped under the spray. The pounding water soothed her aching muscles and she forced herself to relax. The house was progressing, the excavator would begin digging tomorrow, and the concrete foundation would be poured by week's end.

Excitement replaced exhaustion at the thought of beginning to frame. It wasn't going to be a big house, just two bedrooms for now. She could expand later, but it was *her* design—she was actually building her very own house.

Towelling her hair dry, Caitlin stopped to listen. An odd sound drew her to the open window. She waited. She heard it again and grew uneasy. The light was fading, and she knew construction sites were often raided at night to steal expensive supplies. The thought of all her beautiful, stacked wood disappearing made her hurry.

Caitlin pulled on her jeans and grabbed a faded green sweatshirt. She tugged it on as she ran to the door. She paused only to retrieve the flashlight she kept by the door. It was hard to remember there were no streetlights to illuminate the dark.

The night air was cool after the warmth of her shower, but it wasn't the weather that made her shiver. Though she couldn't see anything, she sensed something was wrong.

She shone the huge light around the site but saw nothing amiss. The excavator sat in the middle of the site like some giant metal sleeping dinosaur. The only sound was the continuous pulse of waves lapping against the cliff.

Caitlin thought of Kyle moored on the *Sea Unicorn* in the cove below. Maybe she should call him. But what would she say? "I heard a noise. No, I didn't see anything . . . just heard a noise." Caitlin shook her head as if to convince herself how silly she'd sound. *How do you even knock on the door of someone who lives on a boat?*

The chirping of night bugs brought Caitlin back to the present. She was still standing at the end of the driveway and there was no one around. A sudden feeling of loneliness swept over her. Not nostalgia for the friends and family back east, or sorrow at Aunt Elizabeth's death . . . it was a feeling of complete aloneness. She felt that there was no one she could depend on, or turn to, for help and support.

She had always been independent—too much so, her mother complained, but Caitlin believed needing others was a weakness. Now as she stood beneath the endless bowl of the western sky, watching it slowly fill with stars, Caitlin felt small and alone.

The idea of family and community and continuity of place suddenly seemed essential.

She glanced up at the twinkling stars and turned off her flashlight. She recognized the three stars of Orion's belt and instantly was a child again, listening to Uncle Emmet's voice pointing out the constellations to her. From Orion to the Big Dipper to the North Star, she followed the familiar path on which her uncle had always guided her gaze.

There would be hot cocoa waiting for them inside the cabin and Aunt Elizabeth laughing and telling them to hurry. The stars began to blur as Caitlin's eyes filled with tears. An ache in her chest reminded her how much she missed them, but how could she feel alone surrounded by such strong, fond memories? Caitlin had to smile as she wiped away her tears. She would make new memories to add to the old.

A sudden *crack!* startled Caitlin. She struggled to flip on the flashlight, jamming the switch in her panic. The light surged on, blinding her momentarily, when a deafening roar knocked her to the ground.

She covered her eyes as a gigantic fireball exploded in the lumber pile. An instant later the heat of the flames reached her and she rolled away. A shower of sparks and wood splinters rained down on her where she lay too stunned to move.

She heard her name being shouted from very far off but fire consumed the sound as it sucked in the air around her. Gathering her wits, Caitlin scrambled farther from the blaze. She staggered to her feet just as Kyle reached her.

"Caitlin!" He shouted her name again as a second explosion threw her backward into his arms. Tightening his hold on her, Kyle moved them away from the flames.

Caitlin tried to find her breath since all the air was knocked out of her body by the second fireball.

"Are you hurt?" Kyle shouted over the raging inferno.

Caitlin shook her head, too overwhelmed to speak. She could see Kyle's concern in the orange glow of the flickering flames. The adrenaline coursing through her body made her heart pound and her knees weak. Fear gave way to tears as Kyle wrapped his arms around her.

"It's all right now. You're safe. It's just the wood burning."

Caitlin tried to calm herself. She realized he was right. It was just her supplies. She wasn't hurt, but her body began to tremble in reaction to the threat—someone or something had caused a huge fireball to explode in her woodpile.

The hissing and crackling fire seemed to mock Caitlin and she turned away. The blackened ruins of Aunt Elizabeth's cabin were bathed in a horrible glow, a ghostly reminder of the night it was consumed in flames. Caitlin buried her face in Kyle's chest and willed herself not to cry.

The distant sound of sirens gave Caitlin something to focus on while she collected herself. Stepping back from Kyle, she gave him a smile of thanks. He squeezed her hand once and released it. They both jumped at the sound of someone behind them.

Caitlin smothered a cry as she recognized Sara. She saw the relief on her neighbor's face when she saw that Caitlin was safe.

"The fire department is coming. I called as soon as I saw flames." Sara's voice cracked and she pressed her hand to her mouth. She shook her head as Caitlin moved toward her.

"I'm okay. It's just so much like the night Elizabeth died. I didn't want Pippa to ever see fire again. Now that I know you've safe, I've got to get back to her. Will you be all right?"

Caitlin nodded and Sara disappeared back into the woods. Caitlin watched the light of her flashlight weave through the trees and into the darkness.

The fire trucks arrived with their sirens blaring. Caitlin instinctively drew back from the noise and confusion.

Kyle touched her arm to reassure her. "Go on inside. I'll be there as soon as I check with the fire chief." Caitlin was reluctant to leave so Kyle gave her a gentle push toward the trailer. "Go put the kettle on."

She nodded. *Cups of hot chocolate, that's what Aunt Elizabeth would make.* Caitlin watched Kyle direct the pumper truck to the lumber pile. She turned away and went to wait inside.

The flashing red lights were as bright as the fire itself, and Caitlin let the men's voices drown out the sounds. There was nothing they could do to save the lumber, but at least it was replaceable. She'd talk to the insurance company tomorrow and re-order right away.

In a daze Caitlin filled the kettle and rummaged through the cupboard for instant cocoa. There was no milk but she had marshmallows. The thought struck Caitlin as wildly funny. *Marshmallows. Maybe I should take the bag outside and we could all roast them on the fire.*

Caitlin realized she was feeling a little hysterical and very vulnerable. She was relieved when Kyle knocked on the door and came into the tiny kitchenette.

"The fire's contained. Good thing Bob Reilly is a volunteer fireman. He was able to move the excavator a safe distance away. Luckily most of the wood is burning on the driveway so it can't spread to the trees. How are you doing?"

Caitlin's hand began to shake as she passed him a cup of cocoa. "I'm all right." She avoided looking into his eyes, his concern liable to unzip her composure. She took a sip of cocoa and almost burned her mouth.

"Easy now. Sit down and I'll tell you what the firemen said. They won't know 'til morning what happened, and they may have to call out the arson expert from the city to confirm what they found."

"Arson?" Caitlin interrupted. "What did they find?"

"There was an empty gas can lying behind

the pile, and it didn't come from the excavator. That was the first thing they checked."

Caitlin was speechless. *Arson? It made no sense.* A terrifying thought gripped her, and she was afraid that to speak the idea aloud might make it possible. She swallowed hard and found her voice, though it was no more than a whisper. "Do you think an arsonist also burned the cabin?"

Kyle's handsome face clouded with anger. His fist curled around the cup of hot chocolate. "I'd hate to even consider it. Tonight's fire certainly didn't start from an iron left on, like they thought Elizabeth's did . . . but we can talk to the fire chief about it in the morning."

His face softened as he looked at her and suddenly the trailer felt very small. Caitlin was acutely aware of how the tiny dining area was filled by Kyle's presence. To distract herself, Caitlin focused on her cocoa. She stifled a yawn as the day's events wore down her reserve of energy.

"We should both get some sleep." Kyle was instantly on his feet. "Will you be all right here alone in the trailer or should I stay?"

Caitlin cut him off with a wave. "I'll be fine. I doubt anything else could happen tonight—it's practically tomorrow already. Thanks for coming to my rescue." She could see he was reluctant to leave her alone so she stood up.

"Don't worry about me. It was a scare, but I didn't get hurt."

"No, you just got a little dirty." He reached out and wiped a smudge of soot off Caitlin's cheek.

She could imagine what she looked like after rolling around in the dirt, with her wet hair sticking straight up, wearing her oldest sweatshirt.

"You should try and get some sleep. There's plenty of time to sort everything out." Kyle flashed her his most wistful smile and went to the door. "And I know how hard you're going to make me work tomorrow."

Laughing, Caitlin picked up a marshmallow and threw it at him as he ducked out the door. She took the empty cups to the sink and shrieked at her reflection. It was worse than she had imagined.

She pressed a hand to the cheek Kyle had touched. Despite the drenched fire that was smoking only yards from her trailer, Caitlin felt a warm spark inside: her neighbors were becoming friends. Crawling into her narrow bed, Caitlin knew she didn't have to face tomorrow alone.

Chapter Four

"Caitlin, are you okay?" Pippa's big blue eyes searched around as she called through the screened trailer door. The moment Caitlin opened it, Taffy rushed inside, then out again.

"I'm fine, Pippa. It's nice to see you and Taffy this morning."

"I heard the sirens last night and I was worried. My mom said you were all right but I wanted to see for myself."

"Don't you worry. I must have stacked my

47

wood on an old gas can or something. I'm going to go order more wood now."

"Do you want to come to town with us? We're going to buy me new shoes and Taffy's dog food. And then we're going to the museum. It's fun there!"

"Pippa, time to go." Sara appeared by the door. "Do you need anything from town, Caitlin? It's no trouble."

Caitlin shook her head, amazed at the generosity of her neighbors. Life in the city had made her forget what it was like to know the people who lived beside you.

"I'll be going to town later to re-order wood and talk to the insurance agency. But thanks for the offer."

"Any time. And drop by the museum if you want to see those letters from your great-great grandfather."

"That's a lot of greats. He must be a very old man," Pippa concluded.

"We can figure out how old he would be, if he was still alive, while we're in the car. Wave good-bye to Caitlin."

Pippa waved and ran after her mother with Taffy close behind. The dog stopped once to sniff around the burnt woodpile then raced away from the charred smell.

Caitlin wasn't wearing working clothes this morning. She had dressed for town in one of her business suits. The navy blue jacket was short and the skirt long. It was her favorite outfit for client meetings, because it made her feel powerful and competent—and today it helped offset the part of her that had been scared silly last night.

Today she would deal with the fire chief to find out why the woodpile had burned, then she would set the insurance agent to work. She intended to deal with the lumberyard in person. She also decided to pick up a cellular phone in town so she wouldn't feel so isolated.

A second knock on the door startled Caitlin. She waited for Kyle to call out a hello, but none came. As Caitlin cautiously opened the door, she found a stranger standing there.

Dressed in a boldly checked sport jacket and dress pants, Caitlin thought the man must be one of the arson experts or at least an insurance agent.

"Martin Lloyd, here. Nice to meet you, Ms. Hughes. Sorry it's under such circumstances."

Caitlin shook his hand but quickly let it go. There was a smooth tone in his voice and a false feel to his smile that made Caitlin wary.

"What can I do for you, Mr. Lloyd?"

"It's what I can do for *you*, Ms. Hughes. Here's my card."

Caitlin took the white card and read it: *Martin Lloyd, Real Estate Agent.* She stared at the man in disbelief. "I don't understand."

"I have a buyer for this piece of property. Just name your price. Cash. Immediate sale."

"I have no intention of selling. Where did you get that idea?"

Mr. Lloyd seemed unfazed. "Otter Creek is a small town, Ms. Hughes. I heard about the fire last night and immediately became concerned. After your aunt's death and the cabin fire, I figured you'd be uncomfortable building out here. And my buyer is most anxious if you'd like to sell."

Caitlin handed back Martin Lloyd's business card. "The property is not for sale, and I am very comfortable here. I won't be needing your services, now or later."

"No need to rush to a decision. Keep my business card in case you change your mind." He pressed his card back into Caitlin's hand.

"Your neighbor, Sara Fraser, is seriously considering selling. Two adjacent properties available at the same time would be very attractive . . . you could both make a tidy profit."

"Morning, Martin."

The real estate agent jumped at the sound of Kyle's voice.

"You still here, Dermott? I thought you'd

be off following the fish by now." Martin Lloyd backed away from Caitlin as Kyle stood on the trailer steps.

"Whales are not fish, they're mammals. And the gray ones are still up north. Won't be heading to Baja for another few months." Kyle gave the agent a slight smile that invited a challenge. Caitlin felt a flush of pleasure at Kyle's proprietorial look.

"I'm just on my way." The agent gave Caitlin a curt nod and hurried back to his car.

"Are you thinking of selling after last night?" Kyle's tone grew soft with concern.

"Nope." Caitlin dramatically ripped Martin Lloyd's business card in half. "That man gave me the creeps showing up like that, but I guess he could hardly have called ahead since I have no phone. I'm going to get one in town."

Kyle nodded his approval. "Good idea. Not that a toad like Martin Lloyd would have called. He's been hanging around for years trying to buy up this piece of land, and Sara's next door. He badgered your aunt continually, which is why I wasn't exactly welcoming when I saw him this morning."

"I appreciated the backup. He didn't seem to get the message that I wasn't interested in selling. But he *did* say Sara was thinking of selling . . . could it be true? I haven't known her for very long but she seems happy here."

Kyle shook his head angrily. "He's persistent. He started pestering Sara the day after her husband died, three years ago. That was before I found Otter Creek, but your Aunt Elizabeth was furious at Martin's disrespect for Sara's grief. If she didn't sell then, I'm sure she's not considering it now."

"It never occurred to me that she was a widow. There are so many divorces these days I just assumed Sara was a single mother. How did her husband die?"

"He was a fisherman. A huge storm caught most of the fleet offshore and two boats went down. Three men drowned. Most of the families around here had someone on board."

"How sad." Caitlin couldn't imagine how hard it must have been for Sara. "In the city you never think about the men who catch your fish, or the farmers who grow the crops. Food just comes from the supermarket."

"Speaking of which, I wondered if I could catch a ride into town with you. I'm hoping an order for my darkroom has arrived at the post office. I'll buy your gas since I don't have a car of my own."

"I'm happy to give you a ride. No charge, since my tank is full." Caitlin paused. "How do you manage without a car? I can't imagine life without it."

Kyle shrugged and gave her that sweet smile. "I can take the boat anywhere I want on water—I don't worry too much about land. I can even take my dinghy into town, but it seems a waste of fuel for us to travel separately."

"I'll drive today, if you'll take me for a boat ride another time. I'd love to see the shore from the Strait."

"Deal. We'll wait 'til there're whales, then sail out to meet them."

"Could we?" Caitlin's heart soared at the thought.

"It's a promise. Unless of course my boss won't give me the time off."

"I'm sure you can convince her." Caitlin grabbed her purse and keys. Locking the trailer, she followed Kyle to her car. It was hard not to notice how strong and capable he looked. Caitlin felt a stab of panic as she realized how easy it would be to fall for Kyle Dermott.

"Want me to drive?"

Caitlin knew he was teasing but it would be far too easy to learn to lean on his quiet strength and good humor. She pointed to the passenger side. "You sit there and put on your seat belt. I'm a good driver but my car has a temperament all her own."

"Sort of like its owner." Kyle jumped into the car before Caitlin could reply.

Inside the car they both grew quiet as Caitlin edged by the charred ruins of the lumber pile and the burnt cabin. "I guess our first stop is the fire hall," she said.

Kyle shook his head. "First stop is the gas station."

"But the tank is full."

Kyle held up his hand. "But your car is very, very muddy. There's a car wash behind the station. I'll wash it. You look too nice today to do the dirty work."

Caitlin sensed there was no point in arguing with him. She decided to enjoy Kyle's attention, but she wouldn't let herself come to expect it. This was a man who didn't even own a car. A man who could simply untie a rope and sail off, chasing whales or a pair of eagles. He lived his life in search of the next great photograph.

He had no time to worry about breaking hearts. Caitlin relaxed at the thought. Her heart was too well-protected to be hurt, and Kyle was too busy with his work to think about hurting anyone. She could enjoy his company and let him go when the waves and whales and nature called to his camera.

"What are you smiling about?" Kyle was watching her.

Caitlin felt her cheeks grow warm, anxious that he might have followed her train of thought. The man worked for her and had helped her in an emergency—he hadn't presented himself as an object of romantic interest.

She coughed softly to clear her head. "I was simply thinking how nice it is to have neighbors who care. I realize you and Sara were my aunt's friends but I really appreciate your help."

Kyle grew quiet for a moment and Caitlin grew puzzled. She was surprised when he grew serious.

"I think, Caitlin Hughes, that you've been living in the city too long. Most people care about people wherever they live, but here in a small town you get the chance to meet your neighbors. You'll see the same faces over and over again." Kyle made a face and Caitlin laughed. "Don't get me wrong, I really like it. That's why I return to Otter

Creek every summer. But a new face is a welcome sight—especially one as pretty as yours. People help you because they want to, because you're a nice person."

Now Caitlin felt a blush stain her cheeks. "Thanks for the pep talk. I'm going to need it to face the clerk in the lumberyard and remain calm."

"You'll do fine. Why don't you meet me at Mom's Diner when you're all done and I'll buy you lunch?"

"Just like Mom makes?"

"You got it. Although I don't think there really is a Mom, the food is very good."

"Sounds great. I'll meet you there at noon. I'm going to swing by the museum to see those letters Sara mentioned my aunt donating." Caitlin slowed the car at the post office. "I'll take a rain check on washing the car."

Kyle nodded and opened his door. "If you wait long enough here on the coast, it will rain. It rains every day come winter, but I'm not going to tell you that or it'll scare you off."

"Can't be worse than an Ottawa winter." Caitlin shivered at the memory. "Is that why you go to Mexico each year?"

"The rain here, the whales and sunshine there—it has never been a hard choice before. See you for lunch." Kyle shut the car door and let Caitlin drive away.

The word *before* echoed in Caitlin's ears. *Did he mean before he met her?* There was no time to wonder as she pulled up to the lumberyard.

If she wanted her house built before the winter rains began she had to make them understand how serious she was about building. Caitlin ignored the little voice inside that kept repeating whales and sunshine and Kyle. It was an image she tried to forget but it made such a tantalizing picture she walked into the lumberyard smiling.

Knowing her next stop at the fire house would not be pleasant, Caitlin let herself linger. The idea of finding a stroll through the hardware store an enjoyable event made her laugh at herself. She admired the bins of nails and screws, knowing she would go through boxes of each.

The wood order was easy to replace. The clerk simply hit a button on the computer and the old invoice emerged. Caitlin checked off all the wood items that the fire had consumed. She was delighted when they promised to fill the order immediately and ship it out to her this afternoon.

Caitlin instantly felt better. No one had made her feel like an imposter. The boys in the wood yard had even waved, recognizing her from the delivery the day before. Letting herself feel a confidence she knew she didn't yet have, Caitlin drove to the fire house.

She dreaded what the fire chief might tell her, but she had to know the truth. Had someone deliberately burned her woodpile, or was it some kind of accident? And more pressing, was it linked somehow to the fire that had destroyed Aunt Elizabeth's cabin a few months earlier?

Caitlin's family had accepted that perhaps Aunt Elizabeth had been confused the night she died. She could have left the iron turned on when she left for her quilt meeting but it seemed odd—Aunt Elizabeth wasn't one to worry about wrinkles. And Caitlin was sure she never pressed her dust rags, which seemed to be what started the blaze.

Had someone started the fire, wanting to burn Aunt Elizabeth's cabin for some reason, not knowing she had been rushed to the hospital en route to her meeting? Caitlin shivered at the thought and hoped the fire chief could allay her fears.

Chapter Five

Caitlin pulled up to the small cottage that housed the Otter Creek Museum. She saw Pippa and Taffy playing on the lawn surrounded by old logging machines. They didn't seem like antiques to Caitlin but she kept forgetting how young the settlements on the west coast actually were. The rusting machines were definitely part of the area's history.

"Hi, Caitlin. See my new shoes!" Pippa proudly displayed bright red running shoes. "You better hurry if you want to see inside.

The museum closes for lunch in five minutes. Then we're going home."

"Well I better get going then. See you later." Caitlin didn't even stop to admire the carefully tended garden beds on both sides of the entrance. She pushed open the heavy wooden door and was pleasantly surprised— the museum was light and airy inside.

A small gift shop was off to the left, its shelves lined with locally made jams and dried sea kelp baskets. Off to the right, an open doorway invited visitors into the museum display area. Sitting in between the two areas was Sara.

She smiled as she put down the phone. "Glad you could make it. Do you want the full tour, which takes all of fifteen minutes, or do you want to save it for another day when you need a diversion?"

"Another day. A little bird outside told me you close for lunch in five minutes. And I'm meeting Kyle for lunch at noon."

Sara gave Caitlin a funny smile, almost conspiratorial. "He's a nice guy, isn't he." It wasn't a question, so Caitlin just nodded. "There's a man who needs to settle down. Drifting around in that boat of his seems such a waste. Maybe building your house will make him want to have a house of his own again."

"Again? Hasn't he always lived on the boat?" Caitlin felt like she was prying, but Sara had introduced the subject.

"Not from what your aunt told me. He used to have a huge house and a thriving business. Sold his share to his partner and came west. That's when he bought the *Sea Unicorn* and started living life through his camera. I think it lets him put some distance between himself and real life. Goodness knows life can be hard, but you can't just watch it through a camera lens."

Sara stopped talking, suddenly embarrassed. "Listen to me, carrying on. I just think Kyle needs a good woman in his life . . . and I think that person might just be *you*, Caitlin Hughes. Now I'm going to go find those letters your aunt donated. Why don't you take a look around the gift shop. We have some of Kyle's photographs for sale. He's very good."

Caitlin had to agree with Sara: Kyle's work *was* very good. She was awestruck by the beautifully balanced photographs. There were killer whales frolicking in the cold waters of the Strait of Juan de Fuca, and gray whales lazing in the blue surf of the Baja. A bald eagle soared over treetops with a freshly caught salmon in its talons, while a sleepy owl nestled in the dark shadows of a fir tree. There was a small black bear asleep by a fallen log, and a photo of a deer daintily avoiding thorns to pull a ripe blackberry off the bush.

Caitlin's favorite was a photo of a rock pool with brightly colored anemones and a small hermit crab emerging from its shell decorated with barnacles. *Now here was a creature who understood her feelings about home.* And here was a photographer who understood the everyday life of the natural world.

Even though her trailer was already crammed full of her belongings, Caitlin decided to buy the photo. It was a gift to herself and to her dream. *I'm going to build and decorate my house just like the little hermit crab and his shell.*

"I'm glad you found something because I can't find the letters. Violet is working in the back. I'll go ask her if she's seen them." Sara looked like she was gathering her courage to go into the work area, and soon Caitlin discovered why.

Violet Gibbon's voice carried all the way to the front, and she didn't sound very pleased. "The letters are not available. I don't care if she is family, they are now property of the museum. Tell her to go away, I'm busy."

Sara came out red-faced and empty handed. She was too angry to speak. "I can't believe the nerve of that woman. Museum property. Elizabeth donated the letters to our archives so they would be available to anyone. You of all people have the right to read them. I'm so sorry."

"Don't apologize. Sounds to me like 'a big fish in a small pond' syndrome. Don't make working with her any harder by worrying about me. I'll come back another day and speak to her myself."

Sara shuddered. "I don't wish that on anyone. I've got a better idea. I'll find the letters and photocopy them for you. Then you can avoid dealing with her altogether."

"That would be great, but only if you promise me it won't cause any problems for you."

"Not at all. I'm in all day tomorrow, and Violet's *not*, so I can do it then. I'll drop by your place on my way home and let you know what I find."

"Better yet, just phone me. I've got a cellular phone until the house is built. Let me give you my new number."

Sara scribbled it down as Pippa burst into the lobby. "Mom! I'm hungry. Isn't it time to go home?"

Caitlin glanced at her watch. "It certainly is closing time, and I've got to go meet Kyle for lunch at Mom's. See you later."

Caitlin hurried out to the car chased by Taffy, who then ran back to wait for Pippa at the museum entrance. If Caitlin had half the energy of Taffy and Pippa the house would be built in a week. Luckily it wasn't going to take as long as she feared. The new wood order was being sent out today, and the insurance agent was dealing with the fire department for her and had begun processing her claim.

The fire chief had nothing new to tell her, but he did calm her fears about the two fires being linked. He made her promise not to worry while he continued his investigation. Caitlin let herself relax. She was looking forward to lunch and to seeing Kyle again.

Mom's diner was exactly as Caitlin had imagined it, right down to the blue gingham curtains. There was an old woodstove on display in the back room, and an odd collection of jugs and bottles and pitchers on a shelf running high above the crowded tables.

Kyle waved to her from a booth in the corner. Stepping forward, Caitlin collided with a tall, thin man rushing out the door.

He stammered an apology and bolted away from her as fast as he could. Caitlin was left with the impression of an awkward adolescent caught red-handed, although the man was probably in his thirties. She put it out of her mind as she saw Kyle. *No awkward youth here, Kyle is definitely an adult.*

"It's nice to see a friendly face," she said, sliding into the booth.

"You mustn't mind the fellow who bumped into you. That's Victor Gibbons. He's been lurching through life since before he started shaving."

"Any relation to Violet Gibbons? I heard her today at the museum—she basically refused to let me see Aunt Elizabeth's letters. But Sara is going to take care of it."

Kyle shook his head in disbelief. "I can't believe her gall. Yes, Victor is her son. She has him running in circles—he was called to the phone just before you came in. I expect Violet has summoned him for something."

"Speaking of phones, check this out." Caitlin flipped open her purse and pulled out her new phone.

"Oh good. I'll sleep better knowing you have that." Kyle gave Caitlin a smile that made her stomach flutter. She forced herself to look away from his dark gaze. She studied the menu and told herself the butterflies she was feeling were the result of hunger. "What's good to eat?"

"The daily special is always good. Today it's Irish Stew in a bread bowl."

"Sounds perfect. And I'll have a cup of tea while we wait."

Kyle handed the menus to the waitress and gave their order. Caitlin saw his expression change as the waitress disappeared. Loud voices filled the restaurant and caused Caitlin to turn around.

Martin Lloyd, the real estate agent, came in with Simon Duff, the contractor. Caitlin turned away quickly, not wanting to see either man.

"The two people I'd least like to run into today," she muttered.

"They've gone into the back room to join Ed Wells. He's such a nice guy I wonder how he can stand those two boors."

"Guess it's like you were telling me about a small town—everyone is your neighbor." Caitlin nodded thanks as a steaming pot of tea was set before her.

"More like an unofficial meeting of the Otter Creek Chamber of Commerce. Let's not allow them to spoil our appetites." Kyle cleared space on the table as lunch arrived.

"Smells fabulous." Caitlin's stomach echoed her words.

"If you like this, I might make my own version of Irish stew for you to try. It's made with seafood."

"How is that Irish?" Caitlin had to ask.

"Isn't it enough that the cook is Irish?"

Caitlin had to laugh. "I'd love to try your seafood stew. Any excuse not to cook."

"No, no, you mean any excuse *to* cook. It's always better when you're cooking for more than one person. How about tomorrow night? I'll get the market to set aside fresh prawns, mussels, scallops, and maybe a little salmon or whitefish."

Caitlin licked her spoon in appreciation as she finished her lunch. "Guess we'd better get back to check on how the excavator is doing. He should be finishing up by now." She reached for the bill but Kyle scooped it up.

"I seem to recall inviting *you* to lunch. You can treat next time. Deal?"

Caitlin had to agree. "Deal." She waited by the door as she watched Kyle pay at the counter. Before he could join her, Simon Duff crossed the room.

Holding the door open he nodded to her.

"Heard you had a little trouble last night. Hope you're not too discouraged."

"No, I'm not Mr. Duff. Thank you for asking." Caitlin kept her voice even although her jaw was clenched in anger. She held her smile until the contractor had to let go of the door and continue on to his truck.

Caitlin jumped at a touch to her elbow.

"Are you okay?" Kyle asked.

"I'm just sick of all these local businessmen expressing concern for my business."

"Then it's definitely time to get to work. Want me to drive?"

Caitlin shook her head as Kyle climbed into the car.

"Wait 'til you see me sail my boat. Then you'll know what a good navigator I am."

"I suppose if you can handle a boat, a car must seem small. How big is the *Sea Unicorn*?"

"Thirty feet of smooth sailing. It's a lot like living in your trailer."

"Only three times as big. I should give the

trailer a name—I mean other than the nasty names I called it on the trip out here. We went *very* slow in the mountains. Did you name your boat yourself?"

Kyle nodded proudly. "I did. Have you heard of a narwhal?"

"The whale with the long tusk?" Caitlin began to laugh. "The whale with the long tusk, spiralling like a unicorn horn. Very clever."

"Thank you." Kyle made a small bow. "I thought it only appropriate since I follow the gray whales south each year."

Caitlin felt her stomach drop at his words. *A gentle reminder. He was a free spirit, and come winter he would be gone.*

Shoving her emotions aside, Caitlin turned into her driveway. The huge yellow machine sat in the middle of a giant hole. Caitlin was thrilled. There was enough work here to keep her busy and her mind off Kyle Dermott.

Caitlin's euphoria faded as she got out of

the car. To her amazement there were small, fresh piles of dirt all around the area of the foundation.

She turned to Kyle in confusion but he seemed equally at a loss. *Why would anyone dig little holes all around the huge foundation hole?*

Caitlin bent to look closer. The edges of the hole were sharp and smooth. Shovel marks were clearly visible in the damp, dark earth. Certainly the excavator hadn't caused them.

"I guess I owe Taffy an apology. I thought the dog was digging on my land." Caitlin's voice dropped as she saw something green glittering in the dirt. She gingerly picked up a broken shard of glass that had been unearthed.

"If Taffy didn't do this, then who did?"

Having no answer, Caitlin shook her head, but fear made her knees tremble. *Was someone trying to scare her off the Hughes property?* She shrugged off her worry as the driver of the excavator returned from lunch to finish the job.

Caitlin smiled. "If they want to dig holes on my land, we'll show them what a *real* hole looks like. Starting with one big enough for my house."

Chapter Six

Caitlin almost dropped the dirty dishes from her hands when the phone rang. It took a moment to realize what the sound was, then another to find it in her purse. Her pulse still beating wildly from the surprise, Caitlin answered. "Hello?"

"Caitlin Hughes?" The voice had a scratchy quality that made it hard to identify if it was a man or a woman speaking. Caitlin thought it was a woman.

"Yes. Who is this?" Caitlin was cautious.

"I'm a friend of your Aunt Elizabeth's. I

79

have a message for you from her. Leave Otter Creek now, before it gets dangerous."

Caitlin's first response was anger that someone would claim to be Aunt Elizabeth's friend with a message. That the message was so unpleasant made Caitlin furious. "Is that a threat?"

There was no answer on the other end of the phone, only a moment of silence and then a dial tone. Caitlin punched the hangup button in frustration. Her hand was shaking as she set the phone down.

She couldn't dismiss it as a random crank call. The woman had known both her and her aunt's name. Not that everyone in Otter Creek didn't know that by now.

Caitlin knew a single call shouldn't upset her, but coming so soon after her wood order being cancelled, then burned, and all the strange holes on her site, the phone call seemed ominous.

"A cup of tea is what you need." Caitlin heard her Uncle Emmet's advice as clearly as if he were standing in her tiny kitchen.

She nodded to herself and filled the kettle. She would put the call out of her mind and by morning it would simply be a minor annoyance.

It was probably just someone who heard her name in town today and thought it would be a good joke. *A single phone call was nothing to fret over.*

Caitlin set the kettle to boil. She decided she would take her tea outside and sit at the old picnic table to watch the sun set. She was going to savor every moment of the long summer nights. And no phone call was going to spoil her evening.

Caitlin yanked open an upper cupboard searching for the tea bags when the phone rang again. The sound stirred her fighting instincts and she scooped up the phone prepared to do battle.

"Who is this?"

"Caitlin? It's Sara. Could you come over and sit with Pippa while I take Taffy to the vet? The silly dog has cut her foot on a piece of glass and I can't get it to stop bleeding."

Caitlin could hear the worry in Sara's voice and immediately felt guilty for snapping at the phone. "Of course I can, I'll be right there."

"I called Kyle too since your line was busy. He's going to come and walk you over. Oh, I've got to go. Taffy won't lie still."

Poor puppy, Caitlin thought. She suddenly realized what Sara had said. *Cut her foot on a piece of glass.* Caitlin pictured the shard of green glass she had found earlier in the day. If the dog had been injured from glass from her property, she was really going to feel responsible. She hurried to switch off the kettle and grabbed a sweater on the way out.

She was ready and waiting at the edge of the woods as Kyle climbed up the cliff path. Caitlin felt herself relax as he waved to her. Tension she'd been unaware of melted away.

She was glad of his company as they entered the woods to follow the trail to Sara's house. Dense trees and bushes edged the path. Dark shadows hugged the trunks of the tall fir trees hiding the twilit sky above.

"Sara sounded worried." Caitlin hoped she didn't sound worried herself.

"Doctor Boots is a wonderful vet. He works out of the back of his house so he's always on call. Taffy's in good hands."

The tiny Fraser cabin sat in a clearing of trees. Warm and welcoming light streamed out of the many windows, urging visitors to come inside. Pippa was waiting for them at the door.

She was dressed in her pajamas, but that didn't stop her from rushing outside. "I'll get the car door open."

Sara was inside trying to convince Taffy to stay calm. The dog was so happy to see new people that she tried to leap up, oblivious to her front paw wrapped in blood-soaked towels.

"Shall I come with you to the vet?"

"No thanks, Kyle. Taffy would be too excited by your company—she would jump all over the car *and* you. I've just got to figure out how to get her into the backseat, then she'll settle down."

"I'll carry her out while you get ready. Come on Taffy, old girl." Kyle scooped the dog up in his arms and Taffy began to lick his face.

Caitlin held the injured paw as Sara grabbed her purse. Pippa held the car door open as Kyle slid the dog carefully onto the backseat. Taffy seemed to sense that everyone was trying to help her and rested her head on the seat as Sara got in the car.

"Thanks, I shouldn't be long. Make yourselves at home. There is coffee made. And Pippa, you be a good girl and go to bed with no fuss."

Caitlin held out her hand to Pippa as the car drove away. "Taffy will be fine. Do you want to show me your room?" Pippa skipped along beside Caitlin back to the house.

"I think I'll soak these in cold water before the blood sets." Kyle gathered up the towels scattered on the kitchen floor. "I'll leave you to do tuck-in duty."

"A book! Read me a book before bed." Pippa danced over to heavily laden bookshelves and pulled out a thick red book. "This one."

Caitlin caught Kyle's glance and tried not to laugh. "Not *all* of that one, it looks pretty thick."

Pippa stood looking at them like they had hurt her feelings. "You're a silly goose." She said, and handed Caitlin the book.

"*The Annotated Mother Goose.*"

"There are lots of long poems and lots of short ones." Pippa held up her finger, "but don't just read the short ones."

"Okay. Let's see if my favorite poem is in here. My Uncle Emmet always read it to me every time I visited." Caitlin winked at Pippa. "And it's very long."

Pippa happily climbed into her bed as Caitlin flipped through the book. She gave a triumphant crow when she found the first-

line index. "It's here!" Caitlin tucked Pippa
in under a bright red patchwork quilt, and
began to read.

Come, take up your hats, and away let
us haste
To the Bullfrogs ball, and the Grass-
hopper's feast;
The trumpeter, Gad-fly, has summoned the crew,
And the revels are now only waiting
for you.
On the smooth-shaven grass, by the
side of the wood,
Beneath a broad oak which for ages
has stood,
See the children of earth and the ten-
ants of air,
To an evening's amusement together
repair.
And there came the Beetle, so blind
and so black,
Who carried the Emmet, his friend,
on his back;

And there came the Gnat and the Dragon-fly too,

With all their relations, green, orange, and blue.

And there came the Moth, with her plumage of down,

And the Hornet with jacket of yellow and brown;

And with him the Wasp, his companion, did bring,

But they promised that evening to lay by their sting.

Caitlin paused to look at Pippa snuggled safely in her bed and found her sound asleep. Quietly closing the book, Caitlin switched off the light and closed the door halfway. She found Kyle sitting on the couch with a cup of coffee.

He stretched as he saw her. "Is that how it ends?"

Caitlin sat down beside him and continued to recite:

Then, as the evening gave way to the
shadows of night,
　　Their watchman, the Glow-worm,
came out with his light,
　　So home let us hasten, while yet we
can see,
　　For no watchman is waiting for you
or for me.

Kyle nodded his approval. "You didn't
need the book to finish. I'm impressed."

Caitlin felt a warm flush. "My Uncle Emmet told it to me so many times, I memo-
rized it. I think he liked it because his name
is in it."

"So is mine." Kyle flashed her a grin. "That
part about the Gad-fly. I've been called that
before since I can't seem to settle down."

*Was that another gentle reminder of his
footloose nature?* Caitlin glanced around
the room, anxious to change the subject.
The Fraser cabin was so cozy and comforting, she let herself sink back onto the sofa.

She couldn't help but admire the quilted

cushions in bright colors and patterns scattered all around the room. A glossy book on quilts lay on the coffee table. "Does Sara make all these cushions and covers?"

Kyle held up a pillow from behind his back. "If I recall correctly, this pillow won first prize at last fall's fair. The quilt on Pippa's bed won in the provincial finals. She's very talented, isn't she?"

Caitlin knew nothing about quilting but she recognized the craftsmanship involved. Some of the patterns were very architectural in their layout. Caitlin could imagine drafting out the gridwork of colors but she couldn't fathom the time and skill needed to actually stitch everything together.

She reached for the quilt book to better appreciate Sara's handiwork. Flipping it open to the marked page, Caitlin found a cheery patchwork quilt of reds and browns just like Pippa's bedspread. The pattern's title was appropriately named "The Log Cabin."

She tilted the page to show Kyle. Noticing the bookmark, Caitlin was surprised to see it was one of Martin Lloyd's business cards. Could the real estate agent have been telling the truth? Did Sara really intend to sell?

An even darker thought made Caitlin feel ill. *Was Sara somehow trying to convince her to sell her property as well? Martin Lloyd had implied that two adjacent properties on the market at the same time would be more valuable. Could Sara possibly be the person trying to scare her into selling?*

Caitlin felt a chill as she remembered how Sara had appeared so suddenly out of the darkness the night of the wood fire. Surely her friend had simply come over to make sure she was safe. *And,* Caitlin reminded herself, *it had been Sara who called the fire department.*

At the sound of tires on gravel, Caitlin quickly shoved the card back in place and set the book back on the table. She pushed the unfounded thoughts from her mind. She was surprised to see how dark it had become outside.

Sara followed a limping Taffy into the

house. The dog's front paw was wrapped and taped to three times its normal size. "I doubt this will even slow her down but the vet said it will mend. Did Pippa behave?"

"Sound asleep. She was no trouble at all." As Caitlin gathered her sweater and flashlight, she avoided Sara's gaze in case she noticed her earlier suspicions.

"Thanks so much for coming over. It's one of the hardest parts about being a single parent—there is no one to turn to when you need to deal with the unexpected."

"You can call anytime." Caitlin felt all her doubts dissolve—there was nothing sinister about Sara Fraser. Caitlin had to smile at her new friend. The only thing Sara was guilty of was a little matchmaking when she called both Caitlin and Kyle over to baby-sit together.

Caitlin didn't mind. Kyle took her hand to help her as they stepped out into the dark. The flashlight beam was narrow in the pitch-black and it took a moment for Caitlin's eyes to adjust.

"What were those last lines of the poem? Something about shadows of night?" Kyle asked.

". . . as the evening gave way to the shadows of night, their watchman, the glow-worm came out with his light, so home let us hasten, while yet we can see, for no watchman is waiting for you or for me."

Kyle laughed. "Well, we're too late to still be able to see but it would be nice if there was a watchman. I'll walk you right to your trailer door."

As they emerged from the woods a slight flicker of light caught Caitlin's attention. It was behind her trailer, near the old foundation. A cold shiver washed over her as she stood at the edge of the trees.

"There's someone at the old cabin." Kyle's whisper confirmed her fears. "Stay here." Kyle began to move away when Caitlin caught hold of his arm.

"No way are you leaving me here. If there's someone trespassing I intend to confront them myself." She wasn't going to admit there was part of her that didn't want to be left alone even if it *was* her property.

Kyle's hand closed over her own. His voice was quiet. "Okay but stick close. And if there's trouble get behind me."

Caitlin nodded, even though he couldn't see in the dark. She would never let them become separated.

There were no further lights as they approached the foundation. A sudden loud crash echoed across the clearing. Caitlin tightened her grip on Kyle but he kept walking. The noise had come from the edge of the road.

"They're gone." Kyle shone his light around the charred ruins of the cabin. "That must have been the sound of them leaving. Probably just kids poking around the cabin for fun. It only got dark a short time ago."

Caitlin knew Kyle was talking to comfort her but there was something very scary about having strangers prowling around. She was tempted to mention the telephone call but knew that it would only cause Kyle to worry. And she had no proof it was anything more then a joke, just like whomever was exploring the burnt ruins.

She had to agree. "You're probably right. The news of the fire last night was all over town. It must have made people curious so they came out to look around."

"There's not much else for teens to do in Otter Creek. They don't mean any harm. We'll check in the morning to make sure there is no damage."

"I'm more concerned about someone hurting themselves. I guess I'd better post no trespassing signs and start shutting the gates at night. The last thing I need is an accident to happen while we're building."

"Will you be able to sleep tonight? I can always bunk on the floor if it would make you feel better."

"Thanks for the offer but the trailer is tiny—you would never fit. I think we scared off whoever was here. I doubt they'll return. I'll just leave the lights on to let them know I'm home."

Caitlin glanced at her watch, grateful for the pale green luminous dial. It was almost eleven. "We better turn in, the real work begins tomorrow. If we form up the foundation walls, we'll be ready to pour the concrete."

Kyle waited until Caitlin was safely inside and she had locked the door. "See you in the morning."

Leaving the small interior lights on as she crawled into bed, Caitlin didn't think she would be able to sleep. But as she closed her eyes exhaustion won out over worry.

Her last thought was not the fear she had experienced when she saw the lights in the burnt ruins, but the feel of Kyle's hand holding her own. She let that memory comfort her as she fell asleep.

Chapter Seven

Caitlin woke at first light. She quickly switched off the trailer's lamps, not wanting Kyle to guess she'd left them on all night. Despite all the recent setbacks, Caitlin had an optimistic feeling this morning. She was looking forward to a full day's work.

Dressed and waiting for her oatmeal to cook, Caitlin stepped out into the sunshine. She knew she should wait for Kyle before investigating the old cabin's foundations but she was impatient to reclaim a sense of security by confirming everything was intact.

There wasn't much left for the trespassers to disturb, but Caitlin needed to know there had been no damage. She paused at the edge of the charred ruins.

It was still hard to think about the loss of the cabin and Aunt Elizabeth and Uncle Emmet. Even now Caitlin could picture every room in the house, with the odd mix of furniture tucked into corners and crowded into the small rooms. The wood floor had been worn smooth by many generations of Hughes.

Careful not to cause the blackened timbers to collapse any further, Caitlin climbed down onto the packed earth floor of the old root cellar. Despite the bright light, Caitlin wished she had thought to bring her flashlight. The far corners under the toppled beams were too dark to see clearly.

The smell of burnt wood surrounding her caused a moment of panic as if she couldn't breathe the acrid air a moment longer. She couldn't see anything different about the ruins so she decided to leave. She was ready for breakfast, and Kyle would soon arrive to begin work. Ducking under a fallen beam, Caitlin decided to climb up the far side of the foundation. Her step faltered at the sight of a pile of rock and earth—the corner of the foundation had caved in.

Closer inspection made Caitlin furious. The walls of dry mortar stones had not collapsed naturally, they had been pulled down. Shovel and pick ax marks were clearly visible. The stones themselves were stacked in rough piles as if sorted. Someone had purposefully been digging here last night.

Caitlin's temper overcame her fear. She was so angry she didn't hear Kyle approach until his shadow made her scream.

"Caitlin!" Not waiting for an answer Kyle scrambled into the ruins to reach her. "Are you hurt?"

Shaking her head, Caitlin had to admit.

"No, only embarrassed. I'm sorry I screamed, I didn't hear you coming."

Kyle looked even more concerned. "I've been calling since I found the trailer empty . . . I guess I imagined the worst after last night."

"It *is* worse than I imagined—look." She pointed to the freshly dug earth and stones.

"What's going on here? It makes no sense," Kyle muttered as he studied the crumbling corner. "Unless someone is searching for something they think is buried here."

"Like buried treasure?" Caitlin would have laughed but something serious was going on. "Well, we know for sure it's not Taffy digging. Her paw is cut, and no dog I know digs at stones and then stacks them up."

Caitlin bent to pick up a rock near her foot. She was trying to decide if she should pile it with the other stones or try and place it back in the collapsed wall when she noticed a piece of gray metal in the earth. She let the rock in her hand fall.

"Kyle?" Her voice was a whisper as she touched the metal. "Do you think this is what our mystery digger is after?"

He was instantly kneeling beside her. "There's only one way to find out."

Caitlin laughed as they began to dig. The edges of a box were clear and Kyle began to shift it back and forth to loosen it. Caitlin held her breath in wonder as he tugged it free. A shower of soil and stones fell to the ground as Kyle handed the box to her.

"I believe this is your property."

Her hands trembled with excitement as she held the small metal box. She shook it once to mentally weigh its contents. "It feels empty. What if it's locked?"

Caitlin could scarcely breathe from anticipation, let alone think. She set it down on the pile of rocks and turned to Kyle. His boyish grin made her laugh at their luck. "You open it, I'm too nervous."

"Are you sure?" Kyle seemed reluctant to take the fun away from her.

"Yes. I can't stand waiting but I'm too anxious to open it. You do it."

Without further delay Kyle clicked open the lid. Caitlin was thrilled that the box was not empty, but mildly disappointed to find only a faded photograph.

It was of a tall, elegantly dressed woman in a long white gown, with a huge sun hat in her hands. The camera had caught the hint of a smile, as if she was about to burst out laughing the moment the photograph was snapped.

Caitlin liked the woman's mischievous expression. "She looks like she can hardly stay still for the camera."

"She looks a little overdressed for an outdoor portrait."

Caitlin turned to Kyle, confused by his words. He explained, "Look at her necklace. It's not exactly something you would pick up at a five-and-dime store."

"Oh, it's lovely." There was no mistaking the size and sparkle of the gemstone necklace. "Rubies?"

"More likely emeralds. Rubies would probably appear darker." Kyle turned the photograph over, searching for more clues. "There's something written here but I can't make it out." He shifted into the sunlight and squinted at the words.

Caitlin hurried to join him, the metal box in her hands. She peered around his shoulder at the faded ink. It wasn't a name or a date, and Caitlin laughed in surprise as she read 'The Bullfrog's Ball' scribbled in a shaky hand.

"Do you think there really was a 'bullfrog's ball'? Is that why she's all dressed up?" The idea captured Caitlin's imagination as she pictured the lawn covered with beautifully attired guests dining beneath the trees.

Except the woman stood on recently logged land, by the thinnest sapling Caitlin could imagine. Not the nicest setting for a party. "I wish we knew who this was, or when it was taken."

"I wish we knew why it was hidden in a

strongbox in the cabin foundation wall." Kyle paused. "And who was here last night searching for it?"

Caitlin shivered despite the warm morning sun. Suddenly she remembered the oatmeal bubbling away on the stove and let out a small sigh of dismay.

"My breakfast is probably burnt." The moment the word was out of her mouth, Caitlin regretted it. Standing in the blackened ruins of the cabin with the charred remains of the woodpile nearby, the word 'burnt' left a bitter taste in her mouth.

"Hopefully you don't mean your coffeepot. I rushed out before finishing my second cup." Kyle held out his hand to help Caitlin out of the cellar.

"Fresh pot coming up. And there's hot cereal enough for two since you'll need all your strength today if we start framing the footings." Caitlin was looking forward to doing some physical labor.

*   *   *

Most of the work so far had been coordinating everything she needed, from financing to supplies. And of course the design plans, but that never stopped since there was always a new idea to improve the house as she went along. Good solid work with hammer and nails would help pound away her anxiety, even if they were using air tools and a compressor.

She tucked the photograph safely back in the metal box. "I think I'll take this in to the museum later to see if Sara knows who this might be."

Kyle nodded. "Good idea. And I'll appreciate the early quitting time—I have a feeling you're going to work me very hard for the next few days."

By mid-afternoon Caitlin was ready to quit. She was tired but thrilled with the wooden forms in place. They had worked steadily together and Caitlin was amazed at how quickly the shape of the foundation walls created a real space.

"I'll pick up the iron bars to tie the inner and outer walls together. Then we can arrange a concrete pour for tomorrow afternoon." Caitlin didn't try to hide her excitement.

"And if you'd like a batch of my Irish stew for dinner tonight, I'll call the market and reserve the seafood, if you don't mind picking it up when you go into town."

Caitlin enthusiastically agreed. "You better double your recipe—after this much hard work I'm staring."

"One large Irish seafood stew coming up. Say seven on the boat, tonight?"

"Seven on the boat. Tonight." Caitlin smiled. "I can say it *and* I can be there. Guess I better go wash up if I'm going to stop by the museum."

Caitlin scrubbed herself clean and set out for town immediately. After a quick stop at the building supply store to order concrete she rushed to the museum before it closed.

The dark and quiet interior calmed Caitlin and she let herself slow down. She was happy to see Sara at the information desk and the rest of the museum empty.

"Hi, Sara. How's Taffy doing?"

"It's amazing, she's running normally on only three paws. How is the building going?"

"Really productive." Caitlin couldn't help grinning as she laid the photo on the countertop. "We found this in the old cellar."

"She's lovely. Do you think it's a relative?"

"I was hoping you might know who it was."

Sara carefully studied the photo. "Well, it was taken at your place—the view of the Olympic Mountains across the Strait is almost identical to my view, so that's a start. Hang on." She ducked behind the counter and came up with a pile of paper.

"Here are the copies I made of your family's letters." Sara slid them into a plain brown envelope. "Best be discreet with Violet around."

Caitlin tucked the envelope under her arm just as the door opened and Violet

Gibbons strode in. She gave Caitlin a brief stare and a dismissive sniff.

"Were there any calls for me, Sara?"

"Nothing, Violet."

"What have you got there?" Violet pounced on the photo, her leathery hands like talons. "Where did you find this?" Violet's eyes fastened on Caitlin and demanded an answer.

"I found it on my property." She reached out for the photo. "So it is my property."

Violet refused to release the photo. "This belongs with the other documents from the Hughes family. Your Aunt Elizabeth would want to ensure the family papers are all together, for the good of the community."

Caitlin forced herself to stay calm. "How is it for the good of the community when you refuse to allow me access to my own family's donated artifacts?" Caitlin reached out again and forced Violet to hand over the photo. "I will certainly consider contributing this photo to the museum at a future date—perhaps *after* you provide me with access to the Hughes's letters." Caitlin didn't think about the copied letters nestled under her arm—better to let Violet think she still needed to see them.

Caitlin wanted to see the originals, to feel the crackling paper in her hands, and see the ink as it was written fresh from the pen of her ancestors, faded by all the passing years.

Violet's scowl changed into what Caitlin guessed was a smile. "Of course you can study your family letters. It just wasn't convenient the other day. Let me arrange them for you and we can set up an appointment." The woman's voice was falsely sweet and Caitlin returned the plastic smile.

"Thank you, Mrs. Gibbons. I'll be in touch. And thanks, Sara. I'll give you a call." Ignoring the glare Violet Gibbons gave her, Caitlin gave a little wave with the photo and left.

She could hardly wait to read the bundle of letters Sara had copied. Perhaps they could give some clue as to the identity of the woman in the photo. The smiling face cheered Caitlin as she drove to the fish market.

Wouldn't it be fun to dress in a lovely white gown for a summer social long ago? The Bullfrog's Ball made Caitlin picture long dresses and a swirl of laughter and parasols. She enjoyed her daydream, but it was a relief knowing Kyle didn't expect her to dress quite so elegantly for dinner tonight.

Chapter Eight

"Smells delicious!" Caitlin was comfortably tucked into the corner seat of Kyle's galley watching him add the last few shrimp to the bubbling pot. Kyle moved around his kitchen with an ease that spoke of years of habit. He knew where to find everything he needed and everything was in its place.

The *Sea Unicorn* was as cozy as her trailer, only bigger and much more organized. The boat had storage spots for everything a man would need at sea. Even the bookshelves had rails to securely hold books in place on rough water.

The gentle rocking of the waves against the hull was a pleasant sensation. Caitlin didn't want to imagine how the boat must roll on stormier tides.

The table was set informally but the dishes sparkled in the candlelight of a hurricane lamp. Kyle set a bottle of white wine on the table.

"I apologize for the plastic wineglasses but crystal is not practical onboard."

"Everything seems very practical."

Kyle bowed his head at the compliment. "Everything except the darkroom. Definitely not practical. I had to add extra tanks for water, and extra storage tanks for the chemicals involved to keep them from the bilge system. It would not do to take photos of nature and then turn around and pollute the water while developing them."

"Do you have a portfolio of pictures I could look at after dinner? I loved what I saw at the museum."

Kyle gave a modest grin and pulled a bulging album out from under a bench cushion bin. "Are you sure this is after-dinner entertainment?"

Caitlin clapped her hands in delight.

"Speaking of the museum, how did it go? Any leads on our mystery woman?"

"Well, Sara and I thought it must be a relative of mine, which makes it all the more exciting for me. Violet Gibbons went ape when she saw it and practically refused to hand it back. And Sara came through with copies of the letters my Aunt Elizabeth donated. I'm looking forward to reading them tomorrow after the concrete pour. I can't wait."

"Well, I hope you're ready to eat—the shrimp are done. And they're nothing like the frozen kind you're used to, I bet."

Caitlin gave a contented little sigh. "Fresh seafood is definitely the best part of living on the coast." Caitlin eyed the overflowing stockpot with delight. It was a creamy chowder full of shrimp, scallops, salmon and halibut, with yellow corn and red peppers. "Looks fabulous."

"No compliments until you've tasted it and you're sure I deserve them."

A fresh baguette with butter, a simple salad, and chilled white wine accompanied the soup, making Caitlin's mouth water.

Kyle picked up his glass. "A toast: to a firm foundation for your house, and an answer to your mysterious photograph."

Caitlin laughed at the dull clunk of plastic glasses but said, "hear, hear." In her heart she said, *here, here* for here was where she was building her dream, and here was where her heart had led her.

Kyle's handsome face over the steady candle flame set her pulse aflutter. She took a sip of the cool wine and let him fill her bowl with the steaming chowder.

"You are an excellent cook." Caitlin was pleasantly stuffed by the end of supper. She let out a small groan as Kyle produced a plate of brownies.

"That's not fair. I didn't save room for dessert." She protested as he placed the plate before her. "And they look homemade."

"They *are* homemade. My mother's recipe."

"A secret family recipe?"

Kyle grinned and shook his head. "Nope. The one printed on the back of the chocolate chip package—I just add more nuts."

The kettle came to a boil and Kyle made tea while Caitlin reached for the photo album. She sat flipping through the binder in awe of Kyle's work—and a little disappointed.

He really was good. So good she knew it was something he was meant to do, to follow his dream and the whales. She slowly turned pages and pages of blue water, darkened only by the huge gray whales lounging in the warm Baja surf.

It came as a shock to reach the middle of the book and see the colors change drastically as the photos returned to the Pacific

Northwest. "I see you're back in our neck of the woods. It's so dark and cold-looking. What a contrast."

"These are my most recent photos. No real theme to them. I think I was so happy to be back I started shooting everything in sight."

He pointed to the top of a Douglas fir. "You can't see the nest very well, but here," he turned the page, "you can see the eagle much clearer."

Caitlin laughed. "Did you use a zoom lense or were you up in the tree?"

"I know better than to get too close to nesting bald eagles. They really are something though, aren't they? Although their call is not quite as majestic as they are—it's almost comical."

"But look at them flying." Caitlin was staring at a picture of eagles soaring over the strait. The next photo showed an eagle in flight with a salmon grasped in its talons. The sunlight glinted off the silver scales and the whole photo came alive. "I'd love to see that."

"I expect you will. I took these photos from almost exactly where your house will be. You can sit in your living room and watch the wildlife go by."

Caitlin flipped back a few pages to the first shot of the nest and out into the Strait. "Sara thought the woman in the photo we found was standing on my property too, since the background is like her view."

Staring at Kyle's photo, Caitlin pointed to a thin pole sticking up from the bushes at the base of the tree. "What's this?"

Kyle leaned close and Caitlin instinctively moved back. There wasn't much room in the tiny eating nook so Caitlin pushed the album toward Kyle.

"I don't know. It's not very natural-looking, like a tree branch or a sapling." He got up and rummaged in a narrow drawer. "My one junk space. Here we go." He retrieved a magnifying glass and peered at the stick. "I'd say it's a handle for a shovel."

"Really?"

Kyle nodded and handed her the magnifying glass.

It was definitely a shovel handle, and Caitlin could even see a hand holding it. "Someone's hiding in the bushes with a shovel! When did you take this photo?"

"Just after your aunt died. I guess it was my way of dealing with her death—I wanted to preserve this spot before more changed."

"Look here." Caitlin tapped the very bottom of the picture. "These look like the holes I've been finding all over the lot. If only we could see who is holding that handle!"

Kyle poured her a cup of tea. "That's not a problem. We can blow up the photo and enlarge this area. Maybe then we can see the person hiding there. They can't be clever enough to have covered their face if they were stupid enough to leave the shovel in the air."

"You must have scared them when they were digging." Caitlin took a sip of the fragrant tea. "Do you think they were looking for the box with the photo?"

Kyle paused to chew a bite of brownie. "Well, if they were, I'm glad we found it. But why would they want it? We should figure out where the photo was taken and see if it means anything."

Caitlin licked a chocolate crumb from her fingers. "The person is standing by a tiny tree. But there are *hundreds* of trees along the cliff edge!"

"Yes, but we can line up the background with the view. Besides, it must be the oldest tree on your property since it was standing alone in a clear cut."

Caitlin let herself relax. At least someone had been digging on the property for a while, and not just since she arrived. Somehow it made all the trouble on the site seem less like a personal attack.

"I'll enlarge the photo tomorrow after the concrete pour. You check out the letters to see if you can find anything that would tell us why anyone would search for the photo."

"Sounds like a plan."

"And a good one. More tea?"

Caitlin shook her head. "As tired as I am, too much caffeine this late at night and I may not sleep. Speaking of sleep, I think its time I turned in. Thank you so much for the lovely dinner."

"It's nice to cook for company." Kyle stood. "I'll walk you back up the path."

The night air was crisp and much cooler at the water's edge. Caitlin had remembered her flashlight but the moon was so bright she didn't really need it. Still, she was grateful that Kyle was escorting her back to the trailer. The past few days had left her a little on edge. Knowing someone had been trespassing and digging on her land was an unpleasant feeling.

She took Kyle's hand as he helped her step off the boat and onto the dock. *It was a nice, strong hand. Warm in a comforting way.* She reluctantly let go as she reached the stairs, then chided herself for being so wistful.

It was a perfect night for romance. The moon was almost full, lighting their path. Caitlin was glad the climb to the cliff top was too steep for them to feel like talking. In this kind of mood she was likely to chatter away nonsense that she'd regret in the morning.

The sky was clear, a good sign for tomorrow's workday. That thought brought Caitlin back to herself. Kyle was her hired laborer, and neighbor, nothing more. Glad to have reached the trailer, she pushed all romantic notions out of her head.

"Here we are. Do you really feel comfortable sleeping here?" Kyle sounded unsure. "I don't think anyone will be back tonight digging, there is too much moonlight not to be seen."

"I'm fine." Caitlin held up her key. "Besides, I always lock the door securely."

"Good. I'll sleep better knowing you're safe inside."

Reaching for the door, Caitlin let out a cry of surprise as it swung open at her touch.

Kyle was instantly at her side as they stood in the doorway and stared. Someone had ransacked the trailer. Drawers were dumped and cupboards spilled all over the floor.

Caitlin was speechless. She stood staring at the mess, the floor so completely strewn with her belongings there was no place to even step.

Kyle put his hands gently on her shoulders and edged her behind him. "Wait here." He carefully moved inside and checked the tiny bathroom and sleeping bunk. They both knew no one was there but Caitlin felt better as she watched him.

"Can you see your phone?"

Caitlin surveyed the chaos, trying to remember where she had last seen the phone. "In my purse—which I hope they haven't taken." Looking for one object among everything else helped her focus. She found her leather bag under the kitchen table.

With relief, her hands found her wallet.

No money was missing, all her bank cards were still there, and the phone.

Kyle gingerly took it from her shaking hand. "I'll call the police. Why don't you look around and see if anything is missing."

Caitlin gazed about in disbelief. "I can't think of anything a thief would want to take." She didn't have many valuables with her, almost everything she owned was still in storage until the house was built. Her old tape deck was sitting on the kitchen table, the battered box of tapes she had listened to on her drive across country was upside down on the floor.

"Jewelry?" Kyle was waiting for the police to pick up.

"No. I put everything in a safe deposit box at the bank when I first arrived. All my legal papers, jewelry, passport. There's nothing here except the things in my purse, and they didn't touch it." She shook her head in anger. "Why did they bother to make this mess?"

Kyle's reply was cut off as he reported the break-in.

Caitlin stared at the piles of clothes and magazines, jumbled with canned goods and tea towels, barely recognizing her belongings.

Her eye settled on the happy face magnet smiling back at her from the small refrigerator door. The blank, white refrigerator door. She let out a curse. "They've taken the photo!"

Kyle paused to listen to her so she repeated herself, more angry now. "They stole the photo of my relative."

Kyle reached out to calm her. "Yes. Something is missing, an old family photograph. Value? Probably a few hundred dollars for a collector but it's priceless to my friend. Yes, thank you. We'll be expecting him."

Kyle switched off the phone. "They are sending someone out to check out the damage and make a report. Will you be okay until the patrol car arrives? I want to go get something from the boat."

Caitlin fought down a moment of panic at being left alone. "Of course I will. I can talk to the officer myself."

"I'll be back before they get here. I'll bring back my phone so call if anything makes you nervous."

It seemed silly to use a cell phone when they were within shouting distance but the idea made Caitlin feel better.

"Now lock the door behind me," Kyle said as he left, as if she needed prompting. She shut the door and stared at the mess. Papers were everywhere.

"The letters!" She began to frantically search through the piles for the brown envelope. Relieved, she found them under the kitchen table where her purse had been. She gazed at the blank spot on the fridge. *Why had someone stolen the photo?*

Caitlin had a good idea who had caused all this damage. Surely the answer was in Kyle's photo album: the person crouched in the bushes was searching for something. It must be the stolen photo. An answer that made no sense did not make her feel any better.

A knock at the door made her start but Kyle called out that he had returned. Opening the door, she was surprised to see him wrestling with a small tent. A sleeping bag sat neatly rolled nearby.

"What are you doing?"

"I'm camping outside your door. We've had enough nonsense happening around here, I'm not leaving you alone."

"I can't let you sleep outside."

Kyle laughed and snapped tent poles in place. "I live on a boat. You can't get much more outside than that. Besides, I regularly camp out on beaches whenever I find a nice cove to moor in. I'm just glad it's not winter and raining."

Caitlin's protest was lost in the crunch of tires on gravel.

"The police are here, so no more arguments. They'll agree it's safer for me to hang around."

Caitlin let herself be persuaded. She had not been relishing the thought of a night alone in the ransacked trailer. In the morning, she could face the cleanup, once the day chased away the night shadows. Quietly she thanked Kyle then went to meet the officer to file her complaint.

Chapter Nine

Caitlin continued smoothing the top of the soft concrete while Kyle tapped the sides of the wooden forms to settle the cement. The pour had gone surprisingly well despite the disruption of the night before. Caitlin had been too busy from early morning to give further thought to the robbery.

They had started to work at first light, securing the upright steel bars to keep the forms in place. Caitlin's worst fear was that the form would fail and concrete would pour all over her excavation, an expensive and embarrassing mistake, but the pumper truck had delivered the cement, the walls had held, and there was little more to do but wait until the concrete hardened. She signed the packing slip and watched the truck drive away.

She could barely contain her excitement. The top of the foundation walls were flat and level to set the wood framing on top. This next stage would be fast and gratifying as the walls were erected. Her house was finally taking shape. Little black lines on paper were suddenly concrete walls in the black earth.

"Lunch break?" Kyle flopped down on the grass near his tent.

Caitlin gratefully sank down beside him, ignoring the flecks of concrete splattered all over her clothes. "Now we can take the rest of the day off. It's traditional after a concrete pour."

"Is that because we've worked so hard we've earned a holiday?"

"I think it's more to let the cement dry.

There's not much we can do for a day or two. Then we strip off the bars and wood, and finally get to actually build—walls and doorways and windows."

Caitlin bolted to her feet. "I better order my doors soon or I'll be waiting forever. It's just so hard to believe we've actually started."

"Well, you've certainly faced enough setbacks at the beginning."

"It has been a bit discouraging." She gave a little shrug. "But it won't matter once the house is done." Smiling as she looked at the trailer, Caitlin let out a groan. "Guess I'll be straightening up the mess inside this afternoon."

"Do you want help?"

She shook her head. "Thanks for the offer, but I don't think its much worse than my room used to be when I was in my slovenly teenager years."

Kyle stood up. "I think the best thing for me to do is go play around in the darkroom. I am *very* curious to see who is lurking in that photograph." He rustled around in the tent and emerged with his phone. "I'll have this on, so call even if you just want to talk."

He jogged off to the stairs before Caitlin could reassure him, and herself, that she was fine. Although she had to admit she *was* glad his tent was still here.

Inside the trailer, Caitlin was knee-deep in folding the last of her clothes when the phone rang. She tossed a handful of socks in the air before she recognized her phone's ring. Scrambling to reach it she sent a pile of magazines to the floor, but the rest of the space was finally tidy.

Cautiously she answered. "Hello?"

"It's Kyle. Wait until you see who has been doing your landscape work, shovel in hand. I'm bringing the photo up right now."

Caitlin didn't have a chance to say good-bye but she was too excited to notice. Here at last was proof she wasn't imagining all the minor upsets around her. Caitlin knew exactly what they needed to celebrate. She opened the tiny freezer compartment and was delighted to find a can of lemonade. She was hot and thirsty, and ice-cold lemonade was perfect.

She set the jug and two glasses out on the picnic table as Kyle reached the trailer. It was obvious from his grin he was pleased with himself. He had several photos in his hand.

"Do you want to see, or would you rather guess?"

"You mean I know the person?" Caitlin was puzzled: she knew so few people in town. And almost everyone she had met had been nice. She hated to think someone had been deceiving her all along.

"No guesses." She reached for the photos and gasped. There crouched in the bushes, gripping a shovel, was a man clearly trying to hide. "Who is it?"

"Victor Gibbons."

"Violet's son?" Caitlin looked at the photo again. "He bumped into me that day at the restaurant! He used the phone then ran out the door."

Kyle nodded. "His mother probably told him to get out here and keep searching since we were at lunch."

"And there were fresh holes dug when we got back." Caitlin shuddered at the thought of Victor Gibbons lurking around the edges of her property, sneaking about while she was absent. Worse was breaking into her home—however temporary the trailer was, it was *still* her home. "So is this proof enough that Gibbons did all the other damage?"

"There's a quick way to find out." Kyle flipped out his phone and dialed.

Caitlin didn't listen while Kyle told the police what they had discovered. Her mind was busy sorting out the events of the past few days. What was it about the old photo they'd found that would cause Victor and Violet to trespass and steal it? What were she and Kyle missing? And how would Violet have found out about the photo?

"The letters!" Caitlin spoke out loud just as Kyle got off the phone.

"Constable Wong is going to the museum to ask Violet a few questions. What's this about letters?"

"There has to be something in the letters for Violet to know that the photo existed or that it was important enough to steal—which would explain why she wouldn't let me see them."

"Have you had a chance to look at them at all? We've been so busy."

Caitlin raced into the trailer to retrieve the bundle. Leafing through the papers she had to admire her neighbor's thoughtfulness. "Sara's even put them in chronological order—that should make things easier."

Kyle poured two glasses of lemonade and sat down. "What exactly are we looking for?"

"Oh." Caitlin was chagrined to realize she didn't know. She pictured the photo in her mind. "I guess any mention of a party, since the woman was all dressed up with her fancy necklace."

The last word came out muffled as Caitlin

realized what she was saying. "The *neck-lace*! Kyle, do you think that's what this is all about? The necklace?"

"That would explain why Violet had Victor digging up your lawn. That's a lot of work just to find an old photo." Kyle took a long sip while he was thinking. "I think the photo is just a happy accident. You found it, and once Violet saw it she knew that the necklace was real. Maybe she thought that the photo held some kind of clue. It's certainly odd that she'd have Victor ransack the trailer or try to scare you away with the wood fire, but the lust for precious stones does strange things to people."

"Emeralds, you thought earlier. . . . " Caitlin was absentmindedly thumbing the photocopied letters. "We are looking for mention of a necklace, emeralds, or gems. Or maybe a lawn party or photo session when the picture was taken." She halved the pile and gave Kyle the most recent letters.

The stack she kept for herself began with

the date 1887. The writing was as thin and fine as spider's silk but Caitlin could read it clearly. It was addressed to Amy Hughes from her husband Samuel.

Reading the voices from the past, Caitlin was carried back to the rough life homesteaders faced on the coast: huge trees, almost constant rain, and isolation. She marveled at the causal acceptance of hard physical labor that made up day to day life.

Caitlin read several letters from Samuel to his wife in Vancouver while she was caring for her sick mother. Each letter recounted the daily activities of the children, livestock, and weather but for all their plain language and simple content, Caitlin recognized these were love letters. Samuel's love for the land, for the children, and for his wife shone through every word.

By the fifth letter, Caitlin felt like she had known these distant relatives all her life. She appreciated his gentle humor as Samuel told his wife about their youngest daughter Grace and the chickens. Caitlin worried along with Samuel if the temporary bridge over the creek could stand another spring thaw. She laughed at the antics of the two older boys trying to repair the rabbit hutch.

It was only the sound of a car in the driveway that brought her back to the present. Her heart was pounding at the unexpected arrival but she was relieved to see a police car. Setting a block of wood on the pile of letters, Caitlin rose to greet the peace officer.

"Any luck?" Kyle asked.

"Hit the jackpot." Constable Wong opened a file folder and held up the photo. "This what you had stolen, Miss Hughes?"

Caitlin was thrilled to see the photo again. She was sure this was Amy Hughes, her great-great-grandmother. "It is. Where did you find it?"

"Violet Gibbons had it at the museum— she was photocopying it. Seemed to feel that the museum had a right to the photo." The officer held up his hand to prevent Caitlin from objecting. "I'm not saying she has any claim to this picture, I'm just telling you my impression."

"Did she admit to stealing it?" Caitlin tried to keep her voice light but failed.

"She did."

"She *admitted* it?" Caitlin was astonished.

"She sent her son over to get the photo but they both denied doing any other damage. They said they took the photo off the fridge." Constable Wong paused to see if Caitlin agreed. She nodded. "Then Victor brought it back to Violet. That's all she said happened."

"Did you ask her about Victor digging holes on the property?" Kyle held out the enlargement for the officer to see.

He let out a low whistle. "That's Victor all right, and no doubt about it—it's the same view I'm looking at here." He pointed to the water's edge then held up the old photo. "Same view here too. It almost looks like the same tree, a century later."

Caitlin's hands were itching to hold the

photo again. *Had the police solved more than one mystery? Was the woman standing beside the eagle tree?*

"Violet did mention that Victor might have done a little digging on the property after Elizabeth's death. Said he was gathering native species for planting around the museum before the new owner started building and they were lost."

Caitlin bit back a retort, knowing full well that Violet was lying. There were no plants for Victor to dig, it was all commercial grass that had been seeded in the recent past.

"That would explain the photo wouldn't it?" Kyle was looking at her as he continued. "But what about the fire in the woodpile last week? Surely they are suspects?"

Constable Wong nodded. "I asked them about the fire and the ransacking of the trailer, but they denied any knowledge of either. Victor said he left the trailer exactly as he found it."

The officer paused. "I'm inclined to believe them. It's not something I can see either of them doing. Violet may be a tough old nut and Victor does exactly as she says, but neither would be destructive. Did you want to press charges? They did steal your property."

He handed the photos and the copies back to Caitlin. She clutched them tightly and shook her head. "There's not much point. I've got my photo back. I've started building so there can be no more digging. Is there a way to ensure they don't trespass on my land again?"

The officer scratched his head under his hat. "Well, you can post a 'No Trespassing' sign. Or you could take out a peace bond so that they have to stay away from you. That's a little more involved, but it's possible. I don't think they'll be bothering you again. I gave them a good lecture, should scare some sense back into them. Violet gets a little carried away in her zeal for the community."

Caitlin was willing to let the officer believe his version. She knew how silly her story would sound with its hidden emerald necklaces, a story she wasn't even sure was true.

"Thank you, Constable. I'm content to have my photo returned safely, and I will post a private property sign to discourage intruders. Lemonade?"

The officer declined and walked back to the car. Caitlin waited until he was driving away before she looked at the photo again. She held it up to study the view. The tall Douglas fir that the eagles favored shot sky-ward in the center of the horizon.

Caitlin lined up the sapling in the photo to compare. Her heart sank as she realized it couldn't be the same tree. It was close, but the mountains were not in the same spot.

"Oh, I thought we had solved part of the puzzle. But its not the same tree." Her dis-appointment made Kyle give her a little hug of encouragement.

He held up the original photo he had en-larged, hiding Victor's small figure with his hand. "Constable Wong is right." He pointed to a sprawling oak tree beside the fir. "This oak tree must have been planted, since it's not one of the scrawny native oaks."

Caitlin held her breath as she held up the old photo. The tiny sapling beside the laughing woman had to be the same tree.

"An oak tree!" Caitlin turned the photo over and looked at the writing on the back and laughed. She began to recite:

"Come, take up your hats, and away let us haste
    To the Bullfrog's ball, and the Grasshopper's feast;
    The trumpeter, Gad-fly, has summoned the crew
    And the revels are now only waiting for you
    On the smooth-shaven grass, by the side of the wood,
    Beneath a broad oak which for ages has stood. . . ."

Caitlin shouted the last line as she ran toward the broad oak planted on the cliff edge, nestled beneath the towering firs. "This is it. If I was searching for buried treasure, I'd dig here."

She dared a glance at Kyle and saw his eyes were dancing with as much excitement as she felt. "Shall we dig?"

"You're the boss—I'm just a hired laborer. Don't you mean shall *I* dig?"

Caitlin laughed. "I'll go get two shovels."

Chapter Ten

"Do you think this is crazy? We have no proof that there's anything here to dig for."

"Do you want to stop?" Kyle asked as he flipped another scoop of dirt to the side.

"Nope." Caitlin's answer was more of a grunt as she stomped down on her shovel. With a bone-jarring thud, Caitlin hit another rock. She tried to reposition herself between the oak tree's roots.

"I wish we had a pick ax. This is the biggest rock I've hit yet." She continued to scrape away the dirt, hoping to free the

145

stone. She fell silent as a sharp edge jutted out of the earth. The distinct sound of metal hitting metal convinced her of her find.

"It's another box!"

Together they cleared the remaining dirt from around the four sides. Caitlin was too excited to speak. She barely remembered to breathe as Kyle lifted it from the ground. The only sign that the box had been buried for many years was the faint signs of rust along the hinges.

"It feels heavier than the first box." Kyle extended it to her.

Her hands shaking with happy apprehension, Caitlin took it. She gave the box a slight rattle. Whatever was inside shifted slightly. *How much would a necklace weigh?* She stopped herself from speculating on what might be inside and sat with the box on her lap.

"Do we just open it?"

Kyle was watching her, a huge smile on his face. He gave a shrug. "Why not? There might be nothing inside but dirty socks or broken toys."

Caitlin gave a nervous laugh but felt better. She took a steadying breath and flipped the clasps holding the lid shut. She almost shut her eyes as she lifted the top. Inside, a folded piece of paper lay on top of a bundle of colored cloth.

Caitlin was torn. Read the letter, or unroll the cloth and see what was inside? She could almost hear her parents's voices telling her to slow down and read the enclosed cards before opening her birthday gifts. She reached for the letter.

Carefully unfolding the paper, now damp and freckled with dots of mould, Caitlin recognized the fine handwriting even before she saw the signature. "It's from Samuel Hughes."

"Your great-great-grandfather?"

Caitlin nodded as she read aloud.

My Dearest Amy, I return your beloved stones to their source, the ground. I will bury them as we buried you this spring, so they may rest in peace where no one can covet them. Your beautiful necklace has caused nothing but strife, as family and friends turn against one another hoping to possess a handful of gems.

I know you will forgive me. Your beauty never needed adornment and I know now your grace is greater than any earthly jewels I could have given you.

We can only hope that future generations of Hughes might find the spirit of our love in your necklace and not be consumed by greed for its value.

Your grieving husband, until we are reunited, Samuel Hughes.

Caitlin laid the letter down and wiped tears from her eyes. "Oh, I hadn't thought she'd died first. I mean, I know all of my ancestors are dead, but his loss is so great it hurts to read it."

Kyle reached over and held Caitlin's trembling hand. She gave him a thankful smile.

"I guess that means we know what's in the bundle." Caitlin indicated the metal box with a slight nod.

"Well, get on with it." Kyle motioned for her to hurry. "It's been waiting all these years to be rediscovered. There's a reason you found it."

Caitlin couldn't answer. All her attention was focused on the contents of the box. Slowly she unrolled the cloth to reveal a paisley pattern of pale green, red, and brown. "It's a shawl, I think," she said as a dark brown fringe appeared. She stopped as she reached the very center of the rolled shawl.

The rounded lumps of the necklace were undeniable. She glanced at Kyle for reassurance. He flashed her an encouraging grin and Caitlin unfolded the last curl of cloth. They both gasped in awe.

Lying nestled in the corner of the shawl was a small pile of emeralds. The sun, suddenly free of clouds, caught the gems in a brilliant flash of green fire. Cautiously Caitlin reached out to touch the stones, icy cold from their long internment in the earth. Green light dripped through her fingertips as she held the necklace aloft.

"It really is beautiful." Each stone was the size of a hazelnut, cut and polished so the light danced from every angle. The whole necklace was probably eighteen-inches long. Caitlin couldn't begin to count the number of emeralds.

"Whatever will we do with it?" Caitlin felt mesmerized by the flashing jewels.

"You could begin by putting it on until we can find a safe place to keep it."

"Oh." Caitlin's hands clutched the necklace. "It certainly isn't safe here. Not with the trailer broken into so recently."

She checked her watch. "It's too late to get to the bank and place it in the safe deposit box. Oh, what a worry. No wonder Samuel buried it, it was safer there then anywhere I can think of keeping it."

Kyle gave a small laugh. "No, it's safer in your keeping now that you know it exists. Do you really think Violet and Victor will give up that easily?"

Caitlin held up the necklace again. The sun had gone in and the dark stones were still as beautiful. She shook her head. "If they know we've found it, do you think they'll try to steal it?"

"I don't think so, but I do think the safest place to keep this is on your person and out of sight."

Caitlin shivered at the thought. "You don't think Samuel or Amy will mind?"

Kyle reached for the necklace. "I think they will be happy it has been recovered by a member of the family and not some stranger."

Caitlin held herself still as Kyle draped the necklace in place and secured the clasp. The weight of the stones surprised her but it was a pleasant sensation.

She laughed as Kyle sat back to admire her. "I think I'm a little underdressed for my jewelry." Caitlin touched the stones nervously.

Kyle just shook his head. "They match the color of your eyes. You could wear them with anything and look lovely."

Pleased with his compliment, Caitlin felt herself begin to blush. "Green eyes and red cheeks to match the paisley shawl." Self consciously she gathered up the cloth and the letter.

"Still, I'll be glad when we can get these stones safely to the bank. Wait until my parents and cousins hear about this."

"There's no need to worry. I'll be camping on your doorstep one more night. We can be the first ones in line at the bank tomorrow morning." Kyle grabbed his shovel. "For now, I'm going to fill in this hole."

"And I'm going to find a shirt that will make this necklace less noticeable. Then I guess we should think about dinner."

"How about a real cook-out over the campfire? Then I'll really feel like I'm camping. I have Italian sausages and buns, we can roast them over the fire."

"I'll make a salad. And I still have marshmallows."

Kyle threw his hands up in mock horror. "Just so long as you don't throw them at me again."

"Promise."

"I'll clean up here, then clean up myself."

Caitlin happily returned to the trailer. She placed all the Hughes letters, including the old original one, in the metal box. Not feeling the trailer was secure she decided to lock them in the trunk of her car. She would read through the rest of them after the necklace was in her safe deposit box.

She slammed the trunk closed with a feeling of relief that quickly faded as a car pulled in the driveway. Her hand immediately flew to her throat, but the necklace was carefully hidden.

"Mr. Lloyd. Can I help you?" Caitlin kept her voice cold and unwelcoming, hoping the pushy real estate agent would notice. He didn't.

Smiling broadly, he reached out to shake her hand.

Caitlin pulled back. "Sorry. I've been digging." She held up her hands in apology to show the dirt, all the while conscious of the emeralds tucked inside her collar.

"No problem. I was out this way visiting a client, always looking for new clients." He went to hand her another business card.

"No thank you, Mr. Lloyd. You've already given me a card." Not that she had kept it.

"You have certainly been busy." He dodged around her, heading toward the new foundation. "You're even further ahead then Simon Duff told me. Not a problem though, I can still find a buyer for your property even with the house started. Add plans and it becomes a nice package to sell."

"Mr. Lloyd." Caitlin was on the verge of shouting. "I am not interested in selling. And I would ask you to please leave. I am very busy."

He stopped and turned back to her. Caitlin would never know if her words finally sank in, or if the sight of Kyle racing across the property, a shovel on his shoulder, made Martin Lloyd leave.

"My apologies, Ms. Hughes. I won't take up anymore of your time. Give me a call if you change your mind." He scurried back to his car before Caitlin could tell him she wouldn't be calling anyone but the police if he didn't stop harassing her.

"Are you okay?" Kyle was winded from the run.

Caitlin nodded grimly as she watched the real estate agent's car disappear. "I know good salesmen are aggressive but he gives me a headache."

"You and the rest of the community."

"I was afraid he was going to see the necklace and wonder why I was dressed for digging wearing jewels fit for a ballroom."

"You can dress however you like, and who cares what Martin Lloyd thinks. But I feel better that he didn't see them—that would be the start of a new round of gossip. It will be enough to get them to the bank without the story landing on the front page of the community paper."

"It is news to share with the whole town in time, but I'd like to share it with my family first." Caitlin kept her hand protectively at her throat.

Kyle nodded. "Go in and get dressed for dinner. And I don't mean dressed to match the gems—dress for a marshmallow fight. Consider that a warning."

"Hmm. Perhaps I better eat them all before you get back."

Kyle shrugged. "It won't help. I've got a whole bag of giant colored ones stashed away."

Caitlin had to laugh as he hurried off to the boat. She went inside to bundle up.

The flickering campfire made Caitlin feel cozy despite the cool ocean breeze. The turtleneck shirt and thick sweater she was wearing not only hid the necklace but kept her warm. Overhead the stars twinkled in the clear black sky.

"It will be a nice day tomorrow. The wind has blown all the clouds away." Kyle put another log on the fire, careful to replace the screen that kept the sparks from flying into the trees.

He gave a contented sigh. "I almost feel like I am camping. The sky is so beautiful, I could be anywhere and feel at home."

Caitlin experienced a small shock of reality at his words. *He could be anywhere, at a moment's notice. Simply jump into his boat and sail away.* The thought tugged at her stomach but she shrugged it off. She wasn't going to think about tomorrow. Not while it was still tonight and the company so enjoyable.

"Sara told me you used to live in the city. Do you miss it?"

"No, never. I didn't have time to enjoy all of the wonderful things that went on around me. All I ever saw was my office every day, and I watched my business partner struggle through three marriages and two heart attacks."

Kyle took a long drink of his cocoa. "When I decided to get out I didn't want to sell my share of the company to him. I was trying to protect him, but we had started it together—I couldn't very well offer it to an outsider." Kyle fell silent as he watched a large spark dance skyward then burn out.

"What happened?" Caitlin's voice was quiet in the darkness, the crackling of the campfire and the soft roll of the surf the only other sounds.

"He remarried. Fourth-time lucky it seemed, he was very happy until this past Christmas. The third heart attack was fatal. Now his widow is successfully running the company, and here I am on the west coast."

"Free as a bird," Caitlin offered.

"With a few regrets, but I don't suppose we can live other people's lives for them. We all live with the choices we make."

"Well, I'm glad I chose to come here and build." Caitlin shifted slightly, nervous about Kyle's reaction to her next words. "And I'm glad you're here too. It's important to me that my house is built by people who care about it. I don't mean the quality of building but the spirit in which it's built. Does that sound silly?" Caitlin was relieved as Kyle nodded in agreement with her words.

"No, it doesn't sound silly. It reminds me of that old saying, "A laborer works with his hands but a craftsman works with his hands and his heart." We are creating a wonderful house for you."

Caitlin touched the emerald necklace nestled around her neck. "And having an odd but wonderful adventure."

Kyle raised his mug to toast her words.

Caitlin let the hot chocolate warm her, and let herself savor Kyle's company. He might be gone tomorrow but he was here now and she felt safe.

Chapter Eleven

Caitlin woke after a restless sleep. The necklace had lain heavy on her throat all night; not the weight of the actual stones, but the responsibility that came with them.

Once they were secure in the bank's vault, Caitlin would call her parents and her cousins to let them know what she had found. *Would they begin to argue and covet the gems as her distant ancestors had?* Caitlin shivered at the thought.

She should put the kettle on for coffee but she was too anxious to get to town. She was sure Kyle wouldn't mind—they could always stop for breakfast after the bank.

Caitlin tugged on another turtleneck and then knotted a scarf around her neck to cover the bumps of the necklace. She pushed up the sleeves and hoped she wouldn't get too warm. Luckily it was still early in the day.

Stepping outside, the fresh morning air was reassuring. She heard Kyle whistling as he climbed up the bank from the boat. She had heard him leave earlier to shower and change.

"Ready for our bank run." He saluted her. "Did you sleep all right?"

"Not too badly, considering I'm wearing the family jewels. If this keeps up much longer I'll have to buy a fancy gown to go with them."

"Your nightgown didn't work?"

"Only in the confines of my trailer. It's definitely time to put this green ice on ice at the bank."

Unlocking the car door, Caitlin had a curious sensation. She could picture the house behind her, completely finished and lived in, and as Kyle opened the other car door it felt completely natural. She shook her head to chase away such silly thoughts and focused on the day ahead.

"First stop—the bank," she said. "Then breakfast at Mom's, my treat."

"Sounds good to me."

Caitlin felt lighter the moment the emeralds were off her neck and in the deposit box at the bank. She had actually been able to enjoy her bacon and eggs without having to worry about strangers digging, or stealing, or ransacking her property again.

She and Kyle arrived back at the building site with full stomachs and happy smiles. "We can check the concrete later this afternoon and see if we can strip the forms tomorrow."

"You mean I have a free day today?"

Kyle's gaze scanned the blue sky. "I think I'll go for a sail to clear my head. Care to join me?"

Caitlin was delighted to be invited. They paused for her to grab a jacket and hat, and went to the cliff. A horrible sight greeted them. The *Sea Unicorn* was gone.

With a hollow pit in her stomach, Caitlin could see the boat drifting far out into the channel. Kyle let out a soft curse as he saw the boat's dingy submerged beside the dock.

"Someone has done this. I'll have to borrow a boat from the Cove." He turned to run down the beach path to the resort.

"Here, take the car!" Caitlin tossed him the keys. She heard him pull away as she stood on the high bank, watching the sailboat bob helplessly with the currents.

She was too heartsick to move as she anxiously waited for Kyle to appear far below her. She gave a cheer when she saw a small boat speed from the resort toward the *Unicorn.* It seemed to take forever to reach the sailboat but Caitlin realized it was only a few minutes.

She breathed a sigh of relief as Kyle pulled alongside the unmoored vessel and climbed aboard. She could see the *Unicorn* take hold of its course and begin to motor for home, towing the small boat behind it.

An odd sound behind her made Caitlin freeze. Only the hairs on the back of her neck moved as they stood up in fear. She listened. Again she heard the faint sound of metal against metal, back toward her trailer.

Searching the shadows beneath the trees, Caitlin looked but saw no one. Feeling a little foolish, she stepped out into the sunshine and carefully surveyed the property. Nothing seemed out of place. She forced herself to walk to the trailer. She didn't think anyone was there, but she had to be certain.

At the side of the trailer, her gaze fell on a small panel flapping in the breeze. It was the door to the propane tank. Her heart beat faster as she went to inspect the latch. There were scratches marring the trailer's side where someone had pried the panel open. Her throat went dry at the thought. *Someone had forced open the small door.*

She quickly checked the propane tank. She was not surprised to find that the main control valve had been opened to full, a dangerous accident waiting to happen. Too frightened to be angry, Caitlin quickly shut off the tank.

Had that been the sound she had heard? Was the person responsible for this latest threat nearby? Her heart was pounding so loud Caitlin could barely think. Still she was able to hear the quiet rustle behind her.

Not betraying that she knew someone was there, Caitlin's glance fell on an eight-foot long wooden stud lying at her feet. With one fluid motion she grabbed the board and swung around.

She let out a terrified yell as a man dressed in black leaped from the bushes, his face covered by a ski mask. Caitlin realized her mistake when the intruder grabbed the other end of the board with a fierce tug. If she hung on the man could push her around, if she let go he could use it to attack her.

"Construction sites are such dangerous places." The man's voice was muffled by the mask but Caitlin clearly understood the threat. A dangerous game of push-pull, ensued. Caitlin tried desperately not to be forced to the cliff edge.

"Who are you? The necklace isn't here anymore so you might as well give up!"

The man ignored her and shoved the board harder into her stomach. Caitlin hadn't the strength to try and speak again. Her arms began to ache as she pressed back, but steadily he moved her along the bank.

Caitlin was growing frantic. Far below she could see Kyle sailing closer, but nowhere near close enough to help her.

"Taffy!" Pippa's young voice cut through the clearing, momentarily causing Caitlin to lose her footing and stumble. The deadly board wedged between them held her steady. A new fear seized her: *Pippa must not be placed in danger.*

Before Caitlin could call out an alarm, a gold streak bounced by her and slammed into the attacker. Instinctively Caitlin let go of the board and jumped back to guard Pippa.

The man's anguished howl mixed with Taffy's confused barking made Caitlin stop. Looking back she saw the cliff top empty except for Taffy.

"Pippa!" Caitlin grabbed the girl as she ran by. "Stay here." Her voice seemed to paralyze the little girl but Caitlin was already moving back to the cliff. Pippa watched wide-eyed—even Taffy fell silent at her approach. Holding her breath, Caitlin peered over the edge.

The man lay sprawled on the rocks below, a dark stain against the gray. Caitlin's pulse froze until she saw him move. She knew he wasn't dead when he grabbed his upper leg in pain.

Pippa was suddenly standing beside her, Taffy quietly sitting at the little girl's side. "Guess we better call 911," Pippa said. "I'll go get your phone."

"No!" Caitlin's shout startled both of them. "No, sweetie. I can't let you into the trailer until we know it's safe. The man may have done something. Run home and ask your mom to call."

Pippa was wise for someone so young. Caitlin would have laughed at her composure but she felt sick. *Thank goodness the young had so much energy.* Pippa raced home with Taffy at her heels, while Caitlin wondered if she even had the energy to climb down the embankment.

Was the man still dangerous? His low groans of pain reassured her doubts. He had barely moved except to clutch at his leg. *Probably broken,* Caitlin thought with a pang of relief.

Would he really have thrown her over the cliff if he hadn't fallen? Caitlin shuddered. She searched for Kyle and saw the *Sea Uni-*

corn steadily moving closer. Buoyed by his proximity, Caitlin climbed down the steps to the man's side.

She carefully kept her distance. "Are you hurt?"

The man started to shout at her then painfully stopped. "My leg. It's broken." His words were swallowed by the mask. He angrily ripped it off his head.

Caitlin sat back on the steps in shock. Simon Duff, the contractor, lay glaring at her.

"What is this about?" she demanded. "You're angry because I didn't hire you to build my house?"

Duff looked at her with disgust. "I don't care about a stupid house contract. I'm so busy with bigger projects, your house is a joke." He sucked back the pain and grimaced. "Do you have any idea what we planned to build on this site?"

Caitlin started to speak but decided to let him ramble. "Who is 'we'?"

"Me, Martin Lloyd, and Ed Wells."

Caitlin tried not to show her surprise, hoping to keep him talking.

"We would turn the Cove Resort into the biggest destination on the coast. Waterfront pub, deep-water marina, hundreds of cabins. You sell us the land and we'll give you a fair price."

"Like you did my Aunt Elizabeth." Caitlin's voice was as icy cold as she felt.

Duff shifted uneasily, the pain evident on his face. "If we had known Elizabeth was in the hospital, we wouldn't have had to burn the cabin."

"Meaning you would have burned it, if she had simply gone to her quilt meeting as usual. Where was she supposed to live when she came home?"

"I build great senior citizen homes. We had a nice unit all reserved for Elizabeth to move into."

Caitlin was so angry at the man's callousness she was tempted to kick his injured leg. Instead she stood and watched Kyle approach the dock. She could hear the sirens in the distance, and saw Sara and Pippa standing at the cliff top waiting to guide the ambulance attendants.

There was nothing for Caitlin to do. The hard lump in her throat cut off her tears as she waited. In a daze of grief she walked to the dock.

"Here, catch." Kyle tossed a line to her and Caitlin pulled the rope taut. The *Sea Unicorn* glided into its berth, and Kyle jumped out.

"The ropes were cut," he said, tying everything secure.

"Simon Duff is responsible." Her words were flat and Kyle suddenly looked at her. Wordlessly he reached out and enfolded her in a hug.

"What happened?"

Caitlin began to speak but all she was capable of was loud sobs. As if that broke a spell, shouts filled the air. The entire volunteer fire department, police and ambulance attendants were directed by Sara and

Pippa down the steps to where Simon Duff lay cursing his luck and his pain.

Caitlin could even hear Taffy's barks above the din. She found her tears turned to laughter at the absurdity of it all as Kyle waited patiently, his arms protectively around her.

"Simon Duff burned down the cabin, and tried to push me off the cliff. So that the Cove Resort could expand."

"They want the deep water, don't they?" Kyle was muttering angrily. "Does Ed Wells know about this?"

Caitlin nodded her head against Kyle's chest "He and Martin Lloyd and Duff are in it together." A half sob escaped Caitlin. "Poor Aunt Elizabeth. They burned her house, all her memories and mementos from a lifetime. Gone to their greed."

"Hush, now." Kyle lifted her chin gently with one finger, and gazed into her tear-filled eyes. "It's over now. And you're safe. Elizabeth gave you the most precious thing she had, her land. Now it's time to make your own memories." Closing his eyes, Kyle leaned close and kissed her.

Caitlin let herself relax into his arms and his kiss. Her knees felt weak as the ground seemed to shift under her feet.

"Oh, my." She gazed up at him. "I think the earth moved."

"I would love to take credit for that but its not the earth moving, it's the tide coming in."

Caitlin laughed as the dock swayed again, and Kyle held her steady.

"I love you, Caitlin Hughes." Kyle's voice was no more than a whisper above the noise but she heard it.

"I love you too." She wanted to shout it from the treetops.

Together they turned to watch the rescue team lift a ranting Simon Duff onto a stretcher.

"I guess we better go speak to the police." Kyle held out his hand.

Caitlin took his hand, knowing as one adventure ended, another had just begun.

Chapter Twelve

"Stand still."

"I can't, I'm too excited." Caitlin stood by the oak tree, a white straw hat in her hands, the emerald necklace shining in the afternoon sun."

"You're just going to be a blur if you don't let me focus."

Caitlin was too happy to refuse Kyle anything. She smiled, picturing Amy Hughes's portrait in its silver frame, and struck a similar pose. "I want to put this photo beside my great-great-grandmother's."

"Then stop wiggling and let me take a good photo."

"When have you ever taken a bad shot, Kyle Dermott?"

Kyle smiled at Caitlin's compliment.

"Sara, Pippa! Come and join me in the photo." Caitlin called out to her neighbors.

"More pictures?" Sara shook her head. "Your album is going to be huge."

"Can't be helped when you marry a photographer." Caitlin was grinning. "Okay everyone, smile."

"Taffy, don't chew on that!" Pippa held her bouquet above the dog's head, and Caitlin laughed to see Kyle still snapping away.

Sara went and took the camera out of his hands. "I think you need a few more pictures of the bride and groom. You can't have a whole wedding album with the groom behind the camera."

Kyle set down his other two cameras and smoothed his jacket in place. "Do I look all right?" He asked Caitlin, knowing she would always say yes.

Together they stood at the edge of the cliff, the water sparkling in the late summer sun, surrounded by friends and family, and smiled.

"There." Sara gathered up the cameras. "As your Matron of Honor, I pronounce the photo session over. Go and put these away and come and cut the cake."

"Oh, we need photos of that!" Pippa was adamant.

"Then you'll have to take them for us." Kyle handed her one of the smaller cameras. "We'll be down in a few minutes."

Pippa raced off, followed by Sara's fading shouts to be careful. Caitlin linked her arm in Kyle's and together they walked to their new house.

"Shall I carry you over the threshold?"

"Is that allowed, when we built the house ourselves?"

"Well, this is the first time entering as husband and wife." Kyle lifted her up in his arms, the long train of her wedding dress trailing over his shoulder. With a gentle kick he pushed open the front door and swept Caitlin inside.

"Welcome home, Mrs. Dermott."

"What a lovely house, Mr. Dermott."

Kyle gazed around the empty living room and laughed. "Well, there is a lot of space for my few belongings."

"Just wait until all my furniture arrives from out of storage—the house will feel filled to overflowing." Caitlin gave a contented sigh.

Kyle took her hand. "I'm glad we didn't postpone the wedding until the furniture arrived. I'm happy to camp on the floor as long as we're together."

"No need for that. We're lucky my cousins sent a brass bed as a wedding present."

"All that space will spoil you. The sleeping quarters on the *Unicorn* will seem cramped after the luxury of a queen-sized bed."

"I don't mind sharing close quarters with you." Caitlin gave a little smile.

"Oh, no. I know that look. What are you planning now, Mrs. Architect?"

"Well, I did have a few ideas for my next building project. I thought I'd plan on something less ambitious . . . a little remodeling, perhaps?"

"But the house is perfect the way it is!" Kyle looked confused.

"The house *is* perfect. Exactly as I imagined it, only better because I never imagined having someone so perfect to share it with!"

Kyle pulled her into a hug as Caitlin began to laugh.

"I was thinking of the *Sea Unicorn*. Just a little tinkering with the interior—I figure there will be lots of time to design while on our honeymoon."

Kyle pulled back, looking serious. "You really don't mind leaving your beautiful house so soon after finishing it?"

"*Our* house." Caitlin corrected him. "It will always be our house. And it will always be here for us, wherever we end up. I go where you go."

She grinned. "Besides, after all you and Sara have told me about a west coast winter, I'd rather stay warm and dry watching the whales in Baja."

"Well, your cousin certainly seemed excited to house sit, even without any furniture."

"Kirsten is thrilled—even more so since her boyfriend has managed a transfer with his job. He'll be here before we leave."

Kyle laughed. "I think we can predict the next member of the Hughes clan who will be wearing the family emeralds for their wedding." He touched the gems encircling her neck. "You look lovely today."

"I'm finally dressed up enough to match my jewels! Maybe we need another picture."

"There's no need. I'll remember this day forever."

"And we can forget all the horrible things that happened in the past."

Kyle gave her a reassuring hug. "There's nothing to worry about now. Simon Duff will be charged with arson as soon as he's out of the hospital. He has admitted to burning the cabin *and* your woodpile so there's no fear he will escape punishment."

"Do you think he really would have pushed me over the cliff?" Caitlin shuddered at the thought.

"Constable Wong told me Duff overextended his contracting business. That's why he was so desperate for the Cove Resort expansion to happen—to save himself from bankruptcy. But I don't want to even think about it. I intend to keep you safe until we both grow old."

Caitlin let herself relax in her husband's arms. "Did you hear the latest on Martin Lloyd? Sara told me there were so many complaints about his hard-sell tactics that he's lost his real estate license, and now he's selling used cars."

"He'll probably do very well. I'm just glad he is out of our lives."

"And Flo Wells assured me the Cove Resort will never be expanding. She was so upset to learn that Ed had been duped into thinking I wanted to sell. As Flo said, nobody but her fool of a husband would believe a real estate agent like Martin Lloyd. I'm glad they felt comfortable coming to the wedding today. It almost feels like Aunt Elizabeth and Uncle Emmet are still here when I'm surrounded by friends and family."

"They are here with us, in our memories. That's how people who have touched our hearts live on."

Caitlin clasped Kyle's hand to her heart. "I think mine is so full of loving people it may burst. I'm very grateful to have found you."

Together, they stood gazing out the picture window at the lawn full of happy guests. In the distance the sparkling surface of the water was sprinkled with black dots.

"Orcas! Uncle Emmet told me that it was good luck to see them swim by."

"He must be right. I certainly feel like the luckiest man alive. The orcas will soon head out to sea for winter, and the gray whales down to Baja. We've timed our wedding perfectly."

Caitlin gave her husband a kiss. "We'll follow the gray whales, or go wherever else your heart leads you. My heart will always follow."

Caitlin pointed to a framed piece of stitchery on the wall. "Sara found the perfect wedding gift for us." She read the words, " 'Home is where the heart is'. I thought this house was my heart's desire, but I simply didn't dream big enough. Home is wherever *you* are."

"Then lead the way to the cake, and let's celebrate."

Hand-in-hand, Caitlin and Kyle left their house. Caitlin then realized that the home she had dreamed of building had lived in her heart all along. She'd just been waiting for someone to share it with.